GW01072078

**GIRL 6 MIGHT B**
**DARKER, LESS R**
**OF PHONE SEX P**
**HOME, BUT PEO**
**WITH EXPERIENC** **. . . GET USED TO**
**ANYTHING AFTER A WHILE. MAYBE**
**GIRL 6 WOULD BE BACK SOMEDAY.**

'Call me when you get a private line and some balls. Really, sweetheart, I mean it. You've got some pipes.'

Girl 6 finished her drink and smiled at the compliment. Like Alice, she had fallen into some strange looking-glass world that shared space with the city and neighborhoods she had known all her life. This was definitely a new experience with a type of person she hadn't met before. She was certainly outside of her middle-class Queens background now. Not even NYU, for all its proclamations of worldliness, had ever offered anything like this. Girl 6 was a little repelled – more than a little fascinated.

# J. H. MARKS

# GIRL 6

Adapted from the screenplay by
## SUZAN-LORI PARKS

A SIGNET BOOK

SIGNET

Published by the Penguin Group
Penguin Books Ltd, 27 Wrights Lane, London W8 5TZ, England
Penguin Books USA Inc., 375 Hudson Street, New York, New York 10014, USA
Penguin Books Australia Ltd, Ringwood, Victoria, Australia
Penguin Books Canada Ltd, 10 Alcorn Avenue, Toronto, Ontario, Canada M4V 3B2
Penguin Books (NZ) Ltd, 182–190 Wairau Road, Auckland 10, New Zealand

Penguin Books Ltd, Registered Offices: Harmondsworth, Middlesex, England

First published 1996
3 5 7 9 10 8 6 4 2

TM & © Twentieth Century Fox Film Corporation
All rights reserved

The moral right of the author has been asserted

Set in 10/13 pt Plantin Monotype
Typeset by Datix International Limited, Bungay, Suffolk
Printed in England by Clays Ltd, St Ives plc

Except in the United States of America, this book is sold subject
to the condition that it shall not, by way of trade or otherwise, be lent,
re-sold, hired out, or otherwise circulated without the publisher's
prior consent in any form of binding or cover other than that in
which it is published and without a similar condition including this
condition being imposed on the subsequent purchaser

# CHAPTER ONE

Her face was made up – prepared for the unforgiving scrutiny of the audition's video camera. The director was running behind schedule and Girl 6 had already spent an hour waiting with a dozen other African-American actresses. Some of the women were friends from the 'audition circuit' – groups of actresses who roam from corporate advertising agencies to downtown theater groups. Others were amateurs, given a casting director's phone number during a late night at a club by someone trying to impress them. Girl 6 had reviewed the competition and knew that she had a real shot at the role if only she could get a break. She was an actress. She was trained to assume fictional identities and make them real. It was a goal she had been working toward all her life. Girl 6 knew her job and did it well. But she was an unknown. Just another talented young woman in a city pursuing the same dream as a few thousand others. Girl 6 believed in herself. She was ready to take the next step. No more waiting tables. No more equity waiver productions in the basement of under-attended churches. This was the time. She could be whoever they wanted her to be. Girl 6 was ready.

The director rushed in, greeting Girl 6 with an impolite detachment. He was still reviewing his conversation of ten minutes ago with his manager in Los Angeles. The director's latest and greatest (at least in his mind and therefore in the mind of anybody who worked for him) had just opened big nationwide and people were doing whatever they had to do to work with him. His ego didn't need any additional inflating but there were still plenty of people eager to pump him up. The director took Girl 6's headshot and résumé and had her sized up before his eyes even reached the bottom of the page. 'Okay. You can begin.'

Girl 6 felt the adrenalin rush charge through her body. She

took a deep breath. Holding the oxygen in her lungs for a long moment she stopped herself from hyperventilating. Feeling the first seeping of sweat from her pores, Girl 6 focused, 'centered' herself, and took control of her body. She had a character to play. The character didn't sweat and wasn't nervous. Everything was going to be fine. She had studied her audition piece thoroughly and performed it numerous times in her acting class. She was ready. This was her time. Girl 6 gave the director a calm, subtle smile and then entered her character.

'I want you to know the only reason I'm consenting to this is because I wish to clear my name, not that I care what people think. . .'

If he had been paying attention the director would have seen that she was good – surprisingly good. Instead, the techno chirp of his seven-thousand-dollar Swiss watch reminded him that he was falling further and further behind. There was still a room full of women to be seen. There was lunch with Bob and Jane at Nobu scheduled in less than an hour. The traffic downtown would be hell. He wanted to be on time, his assistant had heard that Edgar might be sitting near them, and it was always a good thing to meet a guy who had just bought one of the largest studios in town. What did this girl think she was doing? This wasn't Shakespeare in the Park. If every girl who walked into this room was going to read a piece he wouldn't get out of here in time for dinner.

'Whoa, whoa, whoa, hold on a minute.'

It took a moment for Girl 6 to stop. She was entirely focused and had lost herself within the role. She wasn't standing in the badly lit, smoke- and sweat-stenched little room. Girl 6 was somewhere else completely.

'Whoa, hold up. Listen to me.'

Girl 6's character slipped away and she woke up to where she was. She didn't understand. What was the problem? The piece was going well. Why was this guy interrupting her? But remembering who she was and what the director expected from her, Girl 6 held her temper. 'Can I finish my monologue?'

The director knew somewhere deep inside that he shouldn't have stopped her. He looked again at his watch, time was running short and whatever else this girl was doing she was definitely wasting his time. Why did all these actors feel he owed them so much? Who were they? It was time for shorthand, time to cut to the chase. 'We're looking for the latest hottest. We're looking for the beauty of Halle Berry, the sexiness of a Jada Pinkett, the soaring voice of a Whitney, can you sing?'

Girl 6 could sing. She loved to sing. Maybe she wasn't a Whitney but she was better than average. Girl 6 had paid part of her way through college singing with a band at school parties. She had done weddings and Bar Mitzvahs. Her favorite gigs were the crowded, open-till-dawn East Village clubs. She had even interviewed to do graduate work at Berklee up in Boston. But she had decided against that, knowing that her real goal was acting. 'I . . .'

The director jumped up from his seat and began to pace nervously around the room. He wasn't used to being interrupted — even when he had asked a person a question.

'Don't talk. Listen. We're looking for the range of an Angela Bassett. We want the total package, somebody who has the total game, if you know what I mean.'

Girl 6 wanted the job. Needed the job. She knew just what to say. The director paused. Thinking that he was awaiting her response, Girl 6 started to speak. 'I . . .'

The director cut her off again. 'Don't talk, listen. I know this person is out there, this talented person exists.' He paused again and looked at her expectantly. Girl 6 had learned her lesson. She didn't say a word. The director was pleased. 'Now you can speak.'

Girl 6 was pissed off now, but kept her anger hidden. She was an actress. She was in control of herself. Girl 6 let the character she was performing in the monologue slide out of her body. She assumed a new persona. Not quite the real Girl 6 who might have told this arrogant Armani fuck where to go. Instead, Girl 6 took on the attitude of someone more forgiving and composed. Give him what he wants. 'Thank you. I've been studying for several years with different teachers. Right now I'm with Diane Moresco at the Performing Place. I've done Off Off-Broadway – *The Homecoming* and *The Piano Lesson*. I had some lines in *Law and Order* but they cut them and just showed Sam Waterson looking at me on a slab at the morgue. I can sing, dance, act. If I get the chance you won't go wrong. I just need a break. Would you let me finish my monologue, then I could read for the part?'

There was a moment of silence when she stopped speaking. The director normally wouldn't have let her talk on as long as she had but he wasn't listening. He was thinking about the model he had slept with the previous night. Shit. What agency had she been with? What was her name? How would he reach her? His growing frustration was calmed when he realized his assistant would have all the details. She had probably already sent the girl flowers and a romantic note. The director snapped out of his reverie and realized that Girl 6 wanted to start her monologue again from the top. He didn't have the time for this. 'Not now. Stand up, face the camera, turn around, slowly, slowly. I . . . we need someone who is oozing sensuality. You can sit.'

Girl 6 did as she was told. She sat.

'Unbutton your blouse, let's see your breasts.'

Girl 6's mouth went dry. She hadn't expected this. Her agent hadn't said anything about nudity. Girl 6 needed this job. Was this for real? If the role involved nudity that was okay with her. It might not be her favorite part of the job but if it moved the story along – if it was integral to the character. Or was this guy getting off on telling women he had just met to take off their clothes? She looked at him. She couldn't tell. Sure, he was a name, a player in Hollywood, but there were plenty of assholes in Hollywood. That wasn't news. 'Is this required of the role?'

The director reacted as though he had been insulted. The inference that his request could be anything but in the legitimate pursuit of 'Art' offended his sensibilities and self-image. The

4

director covered his anger with the guise of an affronted member of the politically correct. 'Yes, didn't your agent tell you? We're being total professionals here. There is nudity required in this role.'

Girl 6 had a choice. Maybe this was legitimate. There were plenty of women outside in the hallway who were more than ready to do exactly what she had just been asked to do. Sometimes it came with the job. On the other hand, maybe this guy just wanted to add to his home video collection. Maybe he liked to sit in his living room with the tapes running and show his friends how powerful he was. All these beautiful women, look at what they did for him. But what was the difference to her? She was an actress. Her body was just a tool. It wasn't her being anymore. When she performed a role her body didn't belong to her. It belonged to the director. For that moment, in that context, she belonged to the person giving the instructions. Girl 6 had to make a quick decision and convinced herself that what she was about to do didn't mean anything. As she unbuttoned her blouse she felt the uncomfortable warmth of shame rising – what would her parents think? But they didn't have to know and she needed this job. Girl 6 forced them from her mind. Nudity had been talked about in class. It had its place in an actor's life. Girl 6 had been in a collegiate version of *Hair*. A friend of hers had been in *M. Butterfly* on Broadway. What she stood to lose compared to what she might gain seemed small. She lowered her blouse and showed the director what he had asked for.

The director turned the camera on, panned down from her face to her breasts, lingered there, and then back up again. 'That's it. Freeze. Don't move.'

Unknowingly, Girl 6 had crossed a threshold. Suddenly she knew that the exposure of her body hadn't been performed in a way that was acceptable to her. As the director started to thank her for coming in, Girl 6 sat for a moment and ignored him. She tried to rein in her emotions. Her heart was flying, her head pounding, and tears surged into her eyes. But she wouldn't show the director how she felt. Instead, Girl 6 focused all her energy on holding herself together. She stood, mechanically buttoned her blouse, and walked out the door without making eye contact, pretending not to notice the director's offered hand.

Another woman, someone Girl 6 didn't know, walked into the audition room as she exited. Girl 6 couldn't hold back her tears any longer. Her makeup was streaked by crying and Girl 6's face became a distorted image. The other women looked away or ignored her as she passed. They felt that if they acknowledged her emotion they would somehow become tarnished by it. They were pros, or they told themselves they were, and if this young woman couldn't handle the pressures of a big-time audition, that was just too bad. If Girl 6 couldn't make the cut then there was just one less person fighting for the role they wanted for themselves. And that would be just fine. Of course, not all the women actually felt that way. In fact, only a few of them did. Underneath their layers of protective self-imagery and rationalization they worried about just what had brought Girl 6 to tears. They felt bad for her. No one liked to see a fellow actor down on her luck. And they felt worse about what lay in store for them when their turn came. Girl 6 passed two friends from an acting class but her look told them not to offer more than a standard-issue greeting. Girl 6 walked out the casting office door into the dirty marble hallway and waited for the elevator to rescue her from her humiliation. She stood alone.

# CHAPTER TWO

Walking through midtown Manhattan, Girl 6 marveled at all the people taking their lunch breaks. To most of them, work was a drudgery, something to be endured until the liberation of the weekend. If they could find a way to avoid it, they certainly would. If they won the lottery, you could be sure that the first thing they'd do would be call their bosses and tell them to fuck off. How many people out of this crowd of thousands fantasized about doing just that? Was there a more common fantasy? How many had already worked out their speeches? How many had visualized sweeping off the papers and junk from the tops of their jealous bosses' desks? How many had fantasized about grabbing the boss by the shirt, scaring him, and then reasserting control over their lives by quitting? Work was a whole different thing to Girl 6. Even if she won the lottery she'd want to act. Even if she had everything she could possibly dream of, she would still want to act. In fact, the dream of being a working, successful actress was the very culmination of her fantasy. Work – acting – wasn't something to be endured. It was something to be cherished and thoroughly enjoyed precisely because it was so incredibly difficult to find. Girl 6 didn't envy the office worker's numbing job description, but she did covet the sense of not always having to scramble to find work.

Girl 6 walked the twenty blocks from the Flatiron District – its rehearsal spaces, advertising agencies, hip cafés, and casting offices – to Midtown. It was a long walk to make in New York, especially on a raw day, but even subways cost money and she had to save any way she could. Normally, despite the cold, she would enjoy the walk, knowing that in Manhattan there are few better ways to spend time than on the city's streets. Today, however, she had no interest in the crowds, no interest in the power architecture of Park Avenue, no interest in the television exteriors being shot near Grand Central. She didn't even have any interest in the passing men. Girl 6 had one thought in her head and that was to kill Murray the Agent.

Not really kill, of course, but Girl 6 was as angry as she had ever been in her life. She wanted to scream at Murray and take her performance to the edge – so close to the edge that he just might think she had lost her sanity and just might pose a threat.

Murray the Agent had signed her a year out of NYU after she appeared in an equity waiver production of *The Seagull* in Chelsea. Girl 6 had played Nina and had gotten good reviews from a local paper, *The Chelsea-Clinton News*. A VH1 art director who lived on Twenty-First Street had seen Girl 6 and lined her up for a cameo in a music video. Somehow, Murray had heard about her, wooed her at a flamboyant meal at Tavern on the Green and signed her to a standard deal. Murray flirted good naturedly with all his attractive clients and would have been hurt if anyone had thought him malicious. Girl 6 and Murray had a running joke about her volatile childhood sweetheart who was now a ranger in the Army's Special Forces. Murray was pretty sure the 'boyfriend' didn't exist, that he was just a product of Girl 6's imagination. But Girl 6 knew Murray wasn't certain and while she knew that Murray was just kidding around – the imaginary ranger was added protection. Girl 6 and Murray had always gotten along during their two years together, but the past was history and Murray had really fucked up today.

Girl 6 entered the grime-scarred, white-brick office building on Forty-Fourth Street between Lexington and Third. A security guard working his second job of the day was yanked from his nap when she passed by. Girl 6 gave him a friendly enough smile and his eyes groped her nearly perfect body. The overweight security guard now had fresh material for his daydreaming. As he sat at his desk, the guard began a sleepy but erotic fantasy incorporating Girl 6, his wife, and his native Mexican village priest. Later, when he got home to the Bronx, his reverie would send his wife to her knees – begging the Lord for absolution for her husband.

Riding up to the sixth floor in the plastic 'wood-paneled' elevator, Girl 6 found no forgiveness for Murray in her heart. Opening his smoked-glass door, Girl 6 stormed past the nasty middle-aged beehive who worked as his secretary. Walking right into Murray's inner sanctum, she found him flossing his teeth. The fatty, mustard-smeared remains of a roast-beef sandwich sat on white waxy paper on his desk. 'Murray, what the fuck are you thinking about? Why didn't you tell me?'

Murray yanked the floss from his teeth and spat a bloody wad into the trash can. 'If I told you, you would have never went. How did you do? Knock 'em dead?'

Girl 6 wasn't prepared to accept business as usual. 'I've never been so humiliated in my life.'

Murray felt equally combative. 'Cut the bullshit. You wanna be a star, an actress, so what, you showed 'em your tits. Big fucking deal. He didn't ask you to fuck him. Did you get the part?'

Girl 6 had expected some embarrassment at least, some sense of contrition. 'I walked out.'

Murray felt the gas rising in his chest. His gut constricted. He chugged a fizziless glass of the morning's dose of Alka Seltzer. Here was this girl, his client, without much of a list of credits, turning down the opportunity to work. Murray had made three calls on her behalf to get her the audition and wasn't happy to have his time wasted. Murray rarely lost his temper and almost never yelled. But this time he did – and regretted his reaction even before he finished shouting. 'You walked out? The hottest director in Hollywood, I get you seen by him and you bolt? You know, maybe you, we should go in another direction, maybe somebody can do better by you. The money you owe me, keep it. This isn't working. I can't take this aggravation, it's too much work.'

Being fired by an agent – no matter how nicely it was put – was a big deal. At that moment, however, Girl 6 didn't care much either way. Murray was not looking out for her the way she felt he should. Girl 6's temper rose. 'Maybe you're right, Murray. But I'll pay you back when I get it.'

Murray had heard this line before, and while Girl 6 was a nice kid he didn't really expect to see his investment back. But his cash outlay hadn't been significant and he wasn't worried about the money. Murray knew that they had just made a mistake and that both were too proud to admit fault. He also knew that the consequences of their blow up would be harder on her than they would be on him.

# CHAPTER THREE

Girl 6 was now looking for a new agent and responsible for getting herself auditions until she was signed. During the next week, Girl 6 hoofed herself back and forth between New York's assortment of advertising agencies, production companies and theatrical agents. Casting calls were normally set up by agents, and Girl 6's status as an unrepresented actress was a liability. Companies that didn't know her told Girl 6 that meetings had to be set up by an agent. Occasionally a humane person would accept Girl 6's headshot and promise to keep her in mind if something came up. Mostly, Girl 6 was looked down upon as an amateur for trying to hustle appointments. The people who knew her from previous auditions and jobs were friendly but secretly concerned that Murray had dropped her. No one believed that she had left his agency voluntarily. She just wasn't successful enough to quit. If she had someone else lined up, that would have been all right. Now, though, they wondered what the problem was with Girl 6. Was she a trouble-maker? A prima donna? She was received more warmly, if superficially, by the different talent agencies that she visited. Agents were always looking out for new, attractive clients, but none of them were in any rush to sign someone who wasn't working. It would have been a different matter if Girl 6 had something to lure them to the contract-signing table with – maybe a shot at a commercial, a small role in a prestigious play. Girl 6's immediate prospects were not especially promising. The agents could afford to sit back and see what happened. If Girl 6 seemed to be closing in on a project, they would be happy to sign her. By the end of every day, Girl 6 was exhausted from looking for work.

Girl 6 had promised herself never to wait on another table. She had waitressed since high school, through college, and for some time after that. The few small acting gigs she'd done had encouraged her to give up restaurant work for good. While the money had always been decent and sometimes even great, Girl 6 found that it just wasn't worth the aggravation. There was something about the way the customers dealt with the people who brought them their dinners. Most of the customers would never talk to a stranger the way they spoke to Girl 6 and the rest of the staff. It seemed to be an unwritten agreement that a waitress or waiter did more than just take orders and bring food out from the kitchen. For many of Girl 6's customers, she was a temporary servant, someone who did exactly what they said, someone who was paid to take shit. Any asshole off the street could walk into a restaurant, get a table, and order another person around for the price of a hamburger – not a bad bargain, no questions asked. If the waitress objected, the manager would be called over and the customer was always right. All the better if the customer/loser was being served by a pretty girl – then there was a whole other layer of frustrations that could be worked out. Girl 6 had decided some time ago that she would rather starve than work the floor again. Girl 6 lived modestly, kept her expenses down and had high hopes for a financially rewarding future.

To make ends meet, Girl 6 was now working nights at the hip Club Zero. Working nine to three checking coats was pleasantly mindless but not entirely without stress. The tips were small and the late-night hours disruptive to Girl 6's efforts to find new representation. The club was filled with smoke, noise, and the bullshit of club people drinking too much and enjoying themselves. Girl 6 was tired of serving other people while they had fun. Girl 6 wanted to be the glamorous woman handing over an expensive coat to be checked, not the lowly creature hoping to earn a dollar for taking it. Her solution was to work all the harder towards her goal.

No moment of the day was wasted. Even time spent on the subway was utilized. When she could get a seat, Girl 6 stuffed envelopes with her headshot and résumé to be mailed to prospective agents. When she wasn't hustling auditions, working at Club Zero, or sending out mailings, Girl 6 made sure she put the time to good use by attending her acting classes at the Performing Place. These sessions working with Diane Moresco and the friends she had made there were the most important hours of her week. The other activities were a form of subsistence, things she had to do to survive. Her work at the Performing Place was what it was all about. The warm-up exercises helped Girl 6 separate herself from her life outside of the small theater. Inside these walls, on this stage, she wasn't an anonymous hat-check girl. Working with these men and women, she wasn't just another envelope with a pretty picture and a list of credits inside. She belonged here and the things she learned from Diane and her friends were the skills and the knowledge that would allow her to reach her goal. They would make her the person she wanted to be.

If Girl 6 had any friends that she would describe as close, it would have been the women from the class. They ranged in age from their late teens to women past the age of retirement. After classes they would often have coffee together at the Greek restaurant on Broadway, around the corner from the Performing Place. Girl 6 didn't even know all of their last names but they shared the same goals and were dependent upon each other to reach them. Working together in a combined effort bred camaraderie, and they often stayed late into the night at the restaurant that never closed.

While Girl 6 had family in the city – her parents and older brother still lived in Queens – she hadn't had much contact with them lately. It wasn't that they were estranged exactly, but Girl 6 felt unfulfilled, dissatisfied with who she was and what she had accomplished. Her parents tried to be supportive but she knew they questioned her career choice. While they wanted her to do what made her happy, they constantly asked if she was all right – was she eating enough? They wanted to see her more often and complained that it was too difficult to reach her by telephone.

Girl 6 shared a hall phone with her neighbors in the apartment building. She didn't have one of her own.

Girl 6 knew that her hard-working parents felt accomplishment was an important part of a person's character. If a person wasn't successful, then failure must be a reflection of that person's personality. Girl 6's parents felt that she should find a 'real' job and have a steady income. Then she could pursue acting in her spare time if she wanted to. Girl 6 spent many nights fantasizing about how proud her parents would be of her when she made it big. She'd buy them a house in the country, maybe far out on Long Island, maybe even the Vineyard. Her mother taught art at a local elementary school and had always dreamed of spending her summer painting landscapes. Girl 6's father was a construction foreman for a large company that built up-scale housing developments in New Jersey and Westchester. He had grown up fishing in his native South Carolina and pulled out his reel and line whenever he had a chance. Girl 6 would buy him a fast boat and the most expensive fishing equipment you could find. Maybe he'd even stencil her name on to the stern of the boat. But until Girl 6 was able to show them how much she had done with her life, she wasn't going to bother them with her failure. Walking through the city she would occasionally see a face that looked like her mother or father. For a moment she'd feel a child's thrill at seeing one of her parents after a separation. Then, Girl 6 would turn away – maybe round a corner she didn't need to take, or go back down the stairs into the subway – even though logic told her that the approaching familiar face probably wasn't someone she actually knew.

Girl 6's monologue had gone well tonight. She thought back to her last audition. If that asshole director had paid any attention she would have had a shot at a real role, not just a skin cameo. As Girl 6 put on her jacket, Diane asked her to stay at the theater for a few minutes after everyone else had gone. Girl 6 told her friends she would catch up with them at the Greek's. She hadn't eaten all day, and suddenly realized she was starving. She looked forward to one of the restaurant's famously generous dinner specials. Fat, lonely Andreas always made sure the cooks overloaded her plate – Girl 6 had roasted chicken and those regressively soothing canned green beans on her mind. It was almost ten o'clock. If she had a big meal now she wouldn't have to eat again until the following night. That would save some money. Maybe she would splurge and have some baklava too.

When the others had gone ahead, Diane sat Girl 6 down and put an arm around her shoulders. Girl 6 knew immediately that something was wrong. Diane was a tough teacher and not given to warmth unless there was bad news coming.

'I can't carry you anymore. You're too behind in the fees.'

Girl 6 had not been able to pay her tuition for a few months. She felt bad but figured that when she had some money she could pay Diane back with interest, maybe even make some sort of donation to the theater itself, some piece of equipment that Diane couldn't yet afford. This was how things were in the acting community – people understood lean times, people cut you slack. Girl 6 and some of the other women had gone through stretches when they couldn't pay for their classes but somehow things had always worked out. Girl 6 was a member of the Performing Place family. You couldn't get rid of family members over something as unimportant as money. They were sisters, artists honing their craft. Girl 6 supposed she could have borrowed the money from her parents but she'd already asked for money for her latest headshots. She couldn't bring herself to ask them for anything more. It wasn't as if her parents were rich – they too were just getting by. Girl 6 was silent.

Diane sat with her a moment offering neither sympathy nor condemnation. The Performing Place was her passion but it was also a business; she had bills to pay. She hated to let finances influence her creative work, but Girl 6 would just have to deal with it somehow. It was nothing personal.

Girl 6 saw her life crashing and burning. This class was the cornerstone of her strength. What would she do without it? How

15

could she get to where she was going? Girl 6 didn't indulge in tears. Stonefaced, she left the theater and deliberately crossed the street so that her friends couldn't see her through the plate-glass windows of Andreas's welcoming restaurant. She didn't want to talk with them. She didn't want to talk to anyone. It started to rain and she allowed herself only a quick look at her friends as they joked and ate their meals. Girl 6 knew that she was going to have to be more frugal than ever before. Walking out of the audition, losing her agent – those were things she could deal with. But losing her class, her friends, her teacher . . . suddenly she was in a very bleak place. Something was changing. There would be no hot dinner and sweet dessert tonight – maybe some saltines. Girl 6 was hungry, but not for food. She was starving, but Andreas couldn't help her.

As the cold rain began to spit down, Girl 6 thought wistfully about a cab but immediately dismissed the idea. Forget the subway, too. Girl 6 knew she wouldn't sleep tonight, and a long walk across Central Park and up Fifth Avenue back to Harlem might help to calm her down. There were no other people on the streets as Girl 6 began the long walk home.

Girl 6 spent the next few days entering a seemingly infinite number of undistinguished office buildings, trying to make contact with someone who could help her find work. Nothing was happening. Leaving a casting office where she had a few friends, Girl 6 noticed a flyer for extras. She was a member of the Screen Extras Guild and had made some good money in the past for not a whole lot of work. Usually being an extra meant interminable boredom, sitting around for days, eating Kraft service meals, and waiting to be living scenery. Girl 6 had done crowd scenes as a teenager for *Sea of Love*, been a hotel worker in *Home Alone 2: Lost in New York*, and been in a number of other films that barely got released. There were worse ways to pay the rent. Usually you got to catch up on the reading you always meant to do and net-worked with other aspiring performers.

Girl 6 had noticed that the gulf between the movie stars whom

16

she had 'worked with' on those pictures and herself had never seemed wider than when they were standing shoulder to shoulder. Even though she had walked past Pacino and stood in the same lobby as Culkin and Pesci, it was at those times that she felt the furthest from her goal. They were all pleasant enough, why shouldn't they be? But actors and extras inhabited different universes. If a star caught a cold you knew that the best doctors at the best hospitals were on standby. No expense would be spared to help them feel and look better. As an extra, if you were hit by a car the second assistant director would just call the Extra's Guild and replace you and that would be it. Girl 6 wasn't naïve; she understood why this was so. No person, however, really considered themselves to be just background, certainly not an ambitious young actress like Girl 6. Still, 'tight' was no longer a strong enough word to describe her financial condition.

Girl 6 turned around, went back to see her friend, and got herself a job playing scenery.

There are few places as cold as downtown Manhattan early in the morning. There is something about the way the wind sweeps in off the various rivers and the Atlantic Ocean, and then swirls around the office towers, that makes the city feel like the Arctic. Making matters worse, Girl 6 was an extra in a movie that was set in the summer. There are few places hotter and muggier than Manhattan in August. There is something about the way the moisture rises from the various rivers and the Atlantic Ocean, and then gets trapped between the office towers. Whatever the cause, the director's instructions were that the scene to be shot occurred during a heat wave.

Girl 6 sat on a bench in frigid Battery Park and rubbed herself so she didn't turn blue. She was wearing just a T-shirt, shorts and sandals. The hundred extras huddled together. Those who were friends rubbed each other to generate some body heat. When the icy wind picked up, those who had just met for the first time quickly eased into a familiarity that only came with approaching hypothermia.

Unfortunately, as sometimes happens, Girl 6's beauty intimidated the people around her and she was left to shiver alone. She had been skiing with her parents in New Hampshire in February, she had skated on Long Island in the dead of winter – and yet Girl 6 had never been so cold before in her life. The conditions were painfully brutal. Girl 6 cried, and her tears froze on her cheeks.

The second assistant director knew the director was a prick. The guy got to sit in his Airstream trailer, kept at a balmy seventy degrees, and came out only to call action and cut. The highly paid prick was his boss, however, and the second assistant director had to make him happy. The second assistant director thanked God that he wasn't an extra and shivered inside his Thinsulate jacket he had ordered from L. L. Bean up in Freeport, Maine. It was supposed to be good up to twenty below zero, and he felt genuinely bad for the extras dressed for a very different time of year. The second assistant director had to force the trigger button on his bullhorn. It had frozen in place. 'All right, people, c'mon, it's ninety fuckin' degrees, please don't look cold. My director is not happy with the background action and that means I'm not happy. If I see anybody who looks like they're freezing, I'm sending you home, no check either.'

Girl 6 had drunk a lot of free coffee trying to beat the cold. She had enjoyed a few minutes of an unconvincing warmth before the chill reasserted itself. Now, she had to go to the bathroom. Urgently. The Porta Potties were across the park and back on the street. If she were to go, the travel time alone would take a few minutes. She was exceedingly uncomfortable and finally arrived at a point where she had no choice but to say something. It was go to the toilet or go where she was. Looking around her, Girl 6 knew she wasn't the only one. She was, however, the only one brave enough to call attention to herself.

'May I go to the ladies room, please?'

The second assistant director wasn't a bad guy and normally such a request wouldn't have pissed him off, but the director had chewed him out after the last take and had even threatened to fire him. The second assistant director had a new baby and couldn't afford to lose this job. He had a million details to keep track of while waiting for the prick to emerge from his climate-controlled trailer. The second assistant director was trying to sort things out in his head. Girl 6's request broke his train of thought. 'Excuse me?'

Girl 6 didn't think it was such a tough question to understand. She was standing right next to the second assistant director and spoke quietly, discreetly. 'I have to go.'

The second assistant director lost his cool. Having had his subservient position shoved in his face by the director, he was ready to assert his own limited authority over the first person who crossed him. Under better circumstances he would have been embarrassed to react angrily – no doubt he would cringe at the memory in the future. The second assistant director screamed at Girl 6 so that every extra, every grip, every gaffer, every bystander could see who was in charge. 'No you can't go to the bathroom. No break. We're ready to shoot and I don't give a fuck about SAG Fuck the Screen Actor's Guild representative. You can pee when I say you can pee!!'

It was no longer the frigid cold that numbed Girl 6. She had arrived at a new low and everyone around her could sense it. Girl 6 thought her humiliation was complete.

That night – after an unmercifully long ten-hour day of shooting – Girl 6 took a subway back to her apartment and soaked herself in a scaldingly hot bath. She was too exhausted, too deadened by the shoot to enjoy the pleasure of the steaming water. She was already running late for her next job. Girl 6 got dressed and hurried back downtown in time to check the first coats of the early customers at Club Zero.

The club was busy as usual and the arrivals brought in a cold draft with them as they entered the building. Girl 6 was convinced that the cold clung to their coats and further chilled the crowded check room. Girl 6's throat was increasingly sour and sore. She had trouble swallowing the tea someone brought her from the bar. Girl 6's head began to spin and the crushing bass from the dance floor caused her real pain with each concussive note. She was devoid of energy, her exhaustion deeper than that brought on by fatigue. Girl 6 was sick but couldn't go home; she needed the tips. After a while, though, the effort barely seemed worth it. Sick as she was, Girl 6's normally cheerful banter and flirtations vanished. She took coats and hung them up and handed people their tickets – no smiles, no jokes, no suggestive looks. The customers tipped her accordingly. It was a shitty end to a shitty day.

The management sent Girl 6 home earlier than usual. She wasn't adding anything to the club's sense of fun and they could see she needed to go straight to bed. A bouncer offered Girl 6 the cab fare home, but got sidetracked by an argument at the front door. Girl 6 couldn't stand being in the club for another minute, accepted the thought for the deed, and walked to the subway. Surprisingly, the cold felt good. At least, away from the stuffiness of the packed club, Girl 6 could breathe. She thought about walking home and realized she was just fooling herself. She just didn't have the energy. Girl 6 trudged down beneath the street and caught a train.

There weren't that many people riding the subway, which was just fine with Girl 6. Unable to stop coughing and sneezing, she felt pitiful. At least there wasn't a crowd to move away from her as if she were Typhoid Mary, no audience for her dripping, congested misery. The roll of the train as it sped uptown made her nauseous. Girl 6 felt like puking all over the shiny new train. It would be the perfect end to one of the worst days of her life. Only when the train pulled to a stop, opened its doors, and took in the chilled winter air did Girl 6 get any relief. Then, halfway to the next station she felt her stomach rebelling again.

After a wrenching succession of full body sneezes, Girl 6 was out of tissues. She looked in her purse for a suitable substitute and found nothing. Girl 6 prayed she didn't sneeze again. Her

20

nose began to run and she had to do something. Girl 6 pulled out her copy of *Backstage* – the New York theater paper – and wiped her nose. She looked around, challenging anybody to condemn her. No one was looking and she felt relieved. At least she was spared this particular humiliation.

The trip uptown was long and Girl 6 was tired. With her head heavy with flu she badly needed distraction. The usual advertising signs were boring. There was no one interesting to look at in the car. It took a moment and then Girl 6 realized that *Backstage* would keep her awake until she reached her stop. She had already read most of the stories and flipped through the paper until she happened across the employment section. A large in-your-face ad caught her attention. 'Mo' money – mo' money – mo' money – mo' money. For nice friendly voices – just talk.'

Money for talking, that sounded like a pretty good deal to Girl 6. In fact it sounded too good to be true. She ripped out the ad and tossed the rest on to the seat next to her. After a moment and a series of racking, convulsive coughs, Girl 6 ripped off a few pages from the paper and kept them as emergency tissues. She felt like shit but at least the ad offered some glimmer of hope. Maybe things would work out. Maybe.

# CHAPTER FOUR

Maybe not. In the morning, after a restless night, Girl 6 woke up and tried to remember why she had felt even vaguely good when she had gone to bed. What did she have to feel good about? What had given her this marginal sense of hope? Sneezing, Girl 6 reached for a tissue and remembered the ad in *Backstage*. 'Mo' money. Just talk.' She was going to check this out.

Girl 6 called and got an address. Trying to make a favorable impression, she spent a lot of time getting ready for the interview that she'd been promised. She walked up the two flights of stairs towards an anonymous-looking business office. Wearing an auburn wig and French-tipped fingernails, Girl 6 was over-dressed for the occasion, but she didn't care. She felt good. A job interview was nothing more than an audition. She wanted this job – whatever it was – but if it didn't pan out, the interview would still stand as more auditioning experience. It was a no-lose situation.

There were a number of women working in a fluorescently illuminated salesroom. All were on the phone receiving calls and describing the services that 1-900-970-WOWW provided. Girl 6 peered in through a large glass window and listened as Salesgirl 1 made her pitch.

'Hey there, Sexy. You've just hooked up with the hottest service around where the talk is always hot and cheap. The cost of this call is a dollar ninety-five a minute, plus a five-dollar connection fee.'

Girl 6 couldn't quite make out what the woman was saying and tapped gently on the glass. None of the salesgirls heard her. Neither did a woman doing bookkeeping. Salesgirl 1 continued her selling. 'Specialty calls are priced accordingly. If you don't

22

want to play with me or if you're under eighteen, please hang up now.'

Girl 6 knocked on the glass with a little more force. The bookkeeper looked up, saw her, and went to open the door. She knew a job applicant when she saw one. They all tended to overdress. Now Girl 6 could hear Salesgirl 1 more clearly. 'But if you're ready, willing, and able, stay on the line and get your hands on the fantasy girl of your choice.'

The bookkeeper had a serious look on her face as she put a finger to her lips, demanding that Girl 6 be quiet and not interfere with the important business going on inside. Girl 6 smiled conspiratorially and put a finger to her lips to show she understood the rules. The bookkeeper led her towards a small adjoining office. Girl 6 listened carefully as they passed Salesgirl 1. 'You've got the right place, sir. We've got several young and attractive ladies waiting to talk with you.' Girl 6 was fascinated by what was going on in the salesroom and stole another quick look before the bookkeeper shut the door behind her.

After talking with the bookkeeper and learning about exactly what sort of business was transacted at 1-900-970-WOWW, Girl 6 finally got the chance for an interview. The bookkeeper ushered Girl 6 into another, equally bland office where she was greeted by Boss 1.

Boss 1 was temporarily involved with her crossword puzzle from *The New York Times*, and Girl 6 had time to look around. There wasn't much to see. The little office was completely drab. Boss 1 had added little in the way of personal effects. The only indication that someone actually occupied the office other than various papers and coffee cups was a large neatly hand-printed sign that read: 'The greatest problem in communication is the illusion that there has been any.' Other than that bit of wisdom, there was nothing on the walls. She stared out a small glass window that overlooked the salesroom. With the glass shut, Girl 6 couldn't hear what was being said, but she watched the saleswomen making their pitches and noted their attitudes, which were something of a contradiction. Both saleswomen were uninterested, paying attention to magazines or painting their fingernails but also ironically enthusiastic and bubbly. Their voices promised both fun and sensual satisfaction.

When Boss 1 filled in the boxes of a particularly troublesome word, she looked up at Girl 6. Girl 6 offered a cheerful, knowing smile. 'I understand this is where a girl can make mo' money.'

Boss 1 looked Girl 6 over. 'If you're over eighteen.'

Girl 6 was certainly that. 'I'm twenty-five years old.'

Boss 1 looked her over again. This time with an appraising sense of surprise. 'You got a young voice. That's good. You're not local.'

Girl 6 protested with a New Yorker's good natured indignation, 'Queens, born and raised!'

'And you're an actress?' Boss 1 put down her crossword puzzle and paid a little more attention to this applicant.

Girl 6 liked Boss 1 for her perceptiveness. 'Nice work when I can get it, yes ma'am.'

Boss 1 was also warming up to Girl 6. 'Good. You've got a smile in your voice. That's good.' It was time to see if this kid knew enough to make some money. Time to see if the smile belonged to a Girl Scout or to someone more sophisticated. 'The caller wants an S&M fantasy. You know what that means?'

Girl 6 smiled that she did.

Boss 1 continued her test. 'You're the mistress, he's your slave. Tell me what you're wearing.'

Girl 6 didn't hesitate; the mistress was just another role. 'Leather bra and hotpants maybe. Some of those high-heeled boots. You know the kind?'

Boss 1 certainly did, but then she glanced down at the next challenge on the crossword and decided to see how quick Girl 6 was. This was no job for someone slow on the uptake. Working the phone meant having to think fast and make the right choices, answer the client's questions and requests successfully. She held up the puzzle. 'Seven letters. "That falling feeling."'

24

Girl 6 hadn't expected the question and hesitated. She didn't like crosswords but her mother always had. It had been part of their Sunday morning ritual when she was in high school to do the puzzle together while her father and brother watched football. Girl 6 hadn't done a crossword puzzle in years but her mind was agile. 'Vertigo.'

Boss 1 hadn't expected the right answer. All she had been really looking for was a halfway intelligent reply. This applicant might work out better than she hoped. It was time to ask more serious questions. 'You like men?'

'Yeah. But my luck's for shit. I'm not getting it in life so I can get it on the job, right?'

Boss 1 approved. This kid was smart, had confidence, and a sense of humor. 'That's right. Okay. You're a dominatrix. Finish it.' Girl 6 didn't even pause for thought. She was used to creating quick character descriptions from improvisational exercises. This was no problem at all. 'Maybe blond hair. Maybe thirty-eight Cs. Good-sized jugs. Big nipples.'

Boss 1 always knew someone who was meant for this job and someone who wasn't. Girl 6 was going to be a natural. 'Good. You going after any other interviews?'

Girl 6 hoped not. The work was unusual enough. She felt comfortable around Boss 1 and the other women she could see working the phones. This would do just fine. 'No other interviews. This is the first and hopefully the last.'

Boss 1 was ready to hire Girl 6 but decided to make the hiring a little more enjoyable by delaying it. 'I can't promise anything but I'll put in a good word. Keep your fingers crossed.'

Girl 6 would have been happy to take the job then and there, but since that wasn't an option she felt she had to check out other opportunities. She was surprised when the address on Fifth Avenue turned out to be in the Empire State Building. Somehow she hadn't thought that such a prestigious building would have tenants who were involved in such a socially unacceptable enterprise.

Boss 2's office was quite a contrast to Boss 1's. The suite was definitely upscale – cherry-wood paneled walls, expensive carpeting, a view across Manhattan east towards Queens where Girl 6 grew up. Boss 2 blended in nicely with his office. Dressed in an elegant suit from Paul Stuart, he was well groomed and appeared to be a successful businessman or attorney.

There were a few not-so-subtle clues, however, that this office wasn't part of a stodgy law firm. Hanging on the walls were numerous photographs of naked women, all of them autographed by the models. Girl 6 didn't recognize any of them – they were beautiful – but none had made it big. She did, however, recognize the faces posing together next to an oiled-up blonde. Girl 6 tried to figure out why Boss 2 would display a picture of presidents Nixon, Ford, and Carter. Surely no one would be gullible enough to believe that Boss 2 and these men were acquaintances. Girl 6 laughed to herself when she noticed that Nixon was looking out of his frame and appeared to be scoping the naked red-headed twins swinging from a trapeze in the next picture. Well, he was called 'Tricky Dick' after all, wasn't he? Boss 2 was finishing a phone call and Girl 6 could hear the moaning and slapping sounds of phone girls 'working' in a nearby office.

Boss 2 was all business – no greeting, no chatting, no pretenses of warmth.

'Talk into this.' He turned on a mini tape recorder. Girl 6 wasn't sure what he wanted to hear. Was she supposed to introduce herself? Boss 2 answered her question. 'Fantasy chat. Go on. Tape's rolling.'

Girl 6 hesitated a moment. Doing this kind of talking in this kind of office with this kind of guy was a big switch from the easygoing camaraderie of her first interview. The situation felt awkward, but what the hell. Girl 6 took on a sugary, sexy persona. 'Hey there. I'm so glad you called. What's your name? . . . Mike? Hey, Mike – uh –'

Boss 2 clicked off the recorder. The truth was he had a slightly more ambitious agenda. 'That's great. We'll give this a listen and letcha know. Are you interested in peep show stuff?'

Girl 6 wasn't sure what he meant. She was here to interview for a phone-sex gig, what was Boss 2 suggesting? Boss 2 saw that she didn't understand.

'You sex 'em on a phone, they can see you, they watch you jiggle but no actual contact whatsoever. Some nudity involved, pay's a lot better. Nice clean work.'

Girl 6 didn't like the sound of that idea at all. She was willing to say whatever a guy wanted to hear as long as she couldn't be seen and he was miles away on the other end of a telephone, but to sit naked in a booth a few feet away from some horny asshole whacking off? She didn't even consider it. There was no chance.

'. . . Uh, no thanks.'

Boss 2 wasn't surprised; she didn't look like the type. Nothing ventured nothing gained. So now it was time for a little personal history.

'You ever married?'

Girl 6 had been and didn't know why it mattered. 'Long time ago. It's over.' Boss 2 said he was sorry. Girl 6 said she wasn't. 'He was a kleptomaniac. A real weirdo.'

Boss 2 didn't want to know more than he had already been told. 'Let's keep it light, okay? You got no experience, right? Okay. We have a training session. We'll teach you the ropes. No problem there. We're seeing a lot of ladies, okay?'

Girl 6 could imagine what Boss 2's 'training sessions' were all about. Everything about Boss 2, his overly designed office, his pictures of former presidents, his nude trophy gallery – all felt wrong. Girl 6 wasn't about to become another body on his wall.

'That's not what I had in mind.'

Boss 2 shrugged. It was all just business to him. As soon as Girl 6 walked out the door, there would be half a dozen more women sitting where she was now. Some of them would be thrilled to share wall space with former leaders of the western world.

After a lunch of spaghetti and canned tomato sauce, Girl 6 changed her outfit and strolled downtown to her next appointment, at Fifty-First Street between Second and Third Avenues. The weather had warmed up. The rain had stopped and Girl 6 felt more hopeful about her situation. Girl 6 wasn't just being carried along by her fortunes or misfortunes. Instead she was aggressively pursuing a new goal. Just by being proactive she felt a good deal better.

Manhattan Follies was an upscale topless bar and Girl 6's next stop. Striptease was in vogue all of a sudden and no longer the domain of tired, sagging strippers with dull eyes. Girl 6 had a glass of white wine – on the house, courtesy of the bartender – while she waited for Boss 3 to see her. An earnest-looking pianist, a kid from Julliard no doubt, tried to keep his attention on his music. He wasn't entirely successful and the performers seemed to enjoy distracting him. Girl 6 figured he was new on the job.

Girl 6 was trying on a new persona for Boss 3. Figuring that vulnerability might have a strong appeal to this sort of crowd – and enjoying the irony of the costume – Girl 6 looked like the girl next door. She was pretty and sweet. Boss 3 was well dressed and uptight. Feeding her toy poodle as she talked, Boss 3's delivery was rapid fire. Girl 6 didn't like the feel of the situation. As soon as she sat down, Girl 6 didn't like Boss 3. Behind them, Asian women danced and performed specialty acts for their patrons. Boss 3 gave Girl 6 some background. 'You got three shifts to choose from. You get paid by the call. You get a bonus if the guy requests you by name. Sit, Trigger. Sit. There you go.'

The little dog did as he was told and received a treat. Girl 6 thought, how nice – the dog gets a bonus too. She wondered if Boss 3 would give her a bonus if she did as she was told. Girl 6 did her best to smile. 'What a sweet thing.'

Boss 3 wasn't interested in what Girl 6 thought of her dog. She ignored the comment and continued on. 'The guys call us up and tell us what they want. Sometimes they want a simple suck and fuck, sometimes they want something a little more elaborate. A very dominant girl *por ejemplo*. You with me?'

Girl 6 understood but did not think she could ever be 'with' Boss 3. There was something unappealing about Boss 3 and her outfit. Girl 6's instinct told her that this was an edgier proposition than the other places she had interviewed. She just didn't know why yet.

Boss 3 plowed on. Nothing got in the way of Boss 3. 'Dildos, chains, toilet training, enemas, the mistress–slave routine, *comprende*?'

Girl 6 offered her standard I-want-the-job line. 'I know I can do this job well.'

Girl 6 was covering her ass; maybe she wouldn't get the job she wanted. Maybe she'd have to work for someone like Boss 3. She didn't like the sound of that prospect, but she knew well enough that you can't always get what you want.

Boss 3 kept on going. She was determined to finish her speech. 'Shitting's really big right now. Guys call up, they want you to shit on them. That's about every fourth or fifth call. They pay by charge card, they call us, we call you, you call them and you chat till they come. It can get a little freaky sometimes. For girls at home anything goes, not like the office girls.'

Girl 6 didn't understand something.

'I call 'em from home?'

'Yep. Collect. Zat a problem?'

If Girl 6 had wanted this job it would have been a problem.

'I share a phone. A hall phone. I don't know if this home stuff is for me. Too heavy starting out.'

Boss 3 wasn't put off and handed Girl 6 her card. She knew a novice when she saw one. Today, Girl 6 might be intimidated by the darker, less restrained version of phone sex performed from home, but people grow jaded with experience. You get used to anything after a while. Maybe Girl 6 would be back someday.

'Call me when you get a private line and some balls. Really, sweetheart, I mean it. You've got some pipes.'

Girl 6 finished her drink and smiled at the compliment. Like Alice, she had fallen into some strange looking-glass world that shared space with the city and neighborhoods she had known all her life. This was definitely a new experience with a type of person she hadn't met before. She was certainly outside of her middle-class Queens background now. Not even NYU, for all its proclamations of worldliness, had ever offered anything like this. Girl 6 was a little repelled – more than a little fascinated.

# CHAPTER FIVE

Girl 6's natural confidence had returned. Although she hadn't had any solid job offers yet, she knew she would soon. Heading home, she stopped at the local Korean deli to get some toilet paper. There always seemed to be a tension surrounding Korean owned stores located in African-American communities. The Koreans didn't trust their Black customers and their Black customers didn't trust the Koreans. Like every other ongoing feud in the world there seemed to be truth, ignorance, and racism in both points of view.

Girl 6, however, got along just fine with the owner of the small store. She treated him with respect and was a regular customer. He treated her with polite deference and made sure that the fruit she bought was the best he had to offer. Inwardly he thought it was a waste for an educated young American woman to try to become an actress. If she were his daughter he would have made sure she became a professional or a business person. Privately, Girl 6 resented the way he treated the majority of his Black customers. The store owner may trust her, but whenever another Black person entered the deli, the owner or his wife or his mother or his son-in-law would watch his every move.

Girl 6 knew about the damage done to Korean stores during the LA riots and she knew about the tragedy of the Korean store owner who shot and killed a Black child not so long ago. While she understood how the tension had grown, she could never really understand it. It didn't take a genius to know that there were Korean people who were assholes and many more who weren't. Identically, there were African-American people who were assholes and many more who weren't. It frustrated her that it was usually only the worst of both that got all the attention. It angered her that weak minds smeared whole races of people for the behavior of a few. Girl 6 was wise enough to be outraged by racism and sophisticated enough to know it would always exist.

At the moment, Girl 6 was having a hard time accepting sides in the ongoing cold grocery war. As Girl 6 reached for a pack of toilet paper with a pair of long 'deli tweezers,' she noticed the deli owner glowering after a young Black man who was examining some fruit. The man was handsome with beautiful hands that lightly brushed over a row of cantaloupes. The deli owner's eyes followed the Black man's hands as they swept over a large watermelon, glided over some red Bartlett pears, past the D'Anjou pears, over the Bosc pears, settled briefly on a navel orange and then flicked it off the shelf and into a pocket. The shoplifter performed the same trick with several apples. The deli owner watched, trying to learn the thief's technique.

Girl 6 tried to defuse the situation. She figured if she could make the shoplifter laugh at the audacity of what he had just done, the young man might just put the fruit back where it belonged. Maybe the Korean owner would let him leave peacefully. 'Stealing is wrong, right?'

The shoplifter knew he had been caught and was about to joke back to Girl 6 when he realized the Korean owner was standing behind him, watching. The two men glared at each other.

Outside the small grocery, people went about their business. People stopped only briefly when the shoplifter burst out of the store and raced down the street as fruit fell from his pockets on to the ground. A moment later the grocer followed and screamed in furious and unintelligible Korean, 'Thief! Thief! Black thief! Black bastard! Black asshole!'

Girl 6 watched from inside the store and paid the owner's wife for her purchases. 'Fuck them both,' she thought to herself. She didn't bother to smile as she received her change. The owner's wife didn't smile either.

# CHAPTER SIX

The New Amsterdam Royal had once been a desirable hotel. Built during the boom of the twenties, it had catered to a wealthy, cosmopolitan Black clientele. Leading actors and musicians of the day would stay only at the New Amsterdam Royal. Hattie McDaniel, Juanita Moore and Dooley Wilson had been guests. The Cotton Club booked all their top performers into the hotel. Rumor had it that late at night, if you passed by just the right room at just the right time, you could still hear the echoes of Fatha Hines, Trummy Young, Pee Wee Jackson and Ray Nance as they relaxed after a show while visiting from Chicago. Today, if you scraped the grime from the floor of the lobby you would find opulent pink Italian marble. If you looked carefully at the yellowed, torn curtains hanging limply in the first-floor windows, you would find a fabric with a weave of hand-painted Chinese silk. Now the New Amsterdam's glory was hidden by decades of neglect. The money had moved elsewhere and it wasn't difficult to get a room nowadays. In the early sixties a new owner had walled off the suites and turned the whole building into single rooms. You could have one for a month, for a week, overnight, or even for an hour. In the 1990s, if any wealthy people visited the New Amsterdam it was just to lament their long-past youth and the hotel's former glory.

Girl 6 had no knowledge of her apartment's history. Her room was a dump that looked better at night when its decay wasn't so apparent. During the day, light poured in through the bent, dusty, venetian blinds that covered windows that probably hadn't been washed in Girl 6's lifetime. The New Amsterdam had two definite advantages, however. It was a relatively safe dump and the rent was cheap.

Girl 6's mother and father hadn't said a word when they

came to see how their daughter was living. Girl 6 knew they were not pleased. After their initial visit she made sure that when they got together they met somewhere else in the city. Girl 6 didn't especially enjoy living the way she did. Yet she was still fresh enough out of college that living the life of a 'starving' artist had its appeal. The shabby room would do until she bought her co-op overlooking the Park. Girl 6 was convinced that her sprawling Central Park West home was not that far off in the future. If only she could catch her break. Girl 6 had already decorated her future home in her mind.

Right now, though, almost anything would have been an improvement. Girl 6 didn't even have a real kitchen. A dorm-sized refrigerator sat in a nook that might have once been a closet. When she ate in, which was most of the time lately, Girl 6 cooked on a hot plate. It took forever to boil a pot of water and she figured it wasn't really worth the effort. If she wanted to bake a potato she used a toaster oven. On the other side of the room was her tiny single bed, with a soft, stained mattress. A multicolored Afghan crocheted by her grandmother covered the bed and kept Girl 6 warm on cold nights when the erratic heating system wasn't keeping pace. Girl 6 had a small black and white television but no cable, no VCR. She had a few books left over from her college days, but most of them were at her parents'. Old copies of *Backstage*, *Premiere* and *People* were stacked on the floor near her bed. Girl 6 invested little of herself in the room. This wasn't where she wanted to be. She would make a real home for herself later – when she had something better to work with. To her the room was simply where she slept, showered and changed. It was never where she actually lived. She wouldn't be here much longer, that was for sure.

In the meantime, there were different ways of escape. If the room's sleeping area and kitchen were unimportant, there was a part of the room that stood as its emotional center. A large old-fashioned vanity table with a beveled glass mirror took up most of one wall. This was Girl 6's 'conjuring' area – where she could transform herself into whoever she chose to become. On the table were a variety of wigs sitting neatly on dummy heads: a long, straight-haired blond wig, a long wavy brunette wig, a jet black bob, and finally an auburn curly-haired wig. Girl 6 also had an armory of other makeup tools: numerous lipstick tubes – reds, browns, purples and pinks, and a rainbow of eye shadows – blues, greens, browns and golds, fake eyelashes, fake fingernails, fake tits.

But all these were just implements for the construction of whatever persona appealed to her on any given day. What really mattered to Girl 6 were the photographs from which she took her inspiration. Girl 6 wasn't religious at all, but her faith in the images taped to her wall bordered upon the devout. In a society where people complained that there were few role models anymore, Girl 6 had no such crisis of belief. Hanging from the walls of Girl 6's ragged little cell was a pantheon of celebrated, beautiful women. Most were performers, and from each Girl 6 gleaned a little something that she insinuated into the creation of her own distinctive character.

Marian Anderson standing on the steps of the Lincoln Memorial in Washington DC. Marilyn Monroe with her skirt blowing up. Bette Davis as the dangerously sexual Jezebel. Billie Holiday singing sadly, angrily and languorously about 'Strange Fruit.' Joan Crawford as the sensually headstrong prostitute Sadie Thompson in *Rain*. Sophia Loren in the sumptuously vivid technicolor of *El Cid*. Josephine Baker in Paris – cheerfully erotic. *Charlie's Angels* trio with big hair, beating up on the bad guys. Lena Horne slaying audiences with the power and purity of her voice. Brigitte Bardot naked somewhere on the Mediterranean and looking like Botticelli's Venus. Harriet Tubman, brave and visionary. Dorothy Dandridge, elegant and playful. Leontyne Price, musical and statuesque. And finally, most important of all, Judy Garland in costume as *The Wizard of Oz*'s Dorothy – lost, innocent and desperate to get where she wants to go.

Girl 6 had just walked inside with her groceries when the hall phone began to ring. She ran back out to answer it, shouting as she went, 'I got it! I got it!' The call wasn't for her. The caller asked for Jimmy. Disappointed, Girl 6 went to her neighbor's door and knocked softly. 'Jimmy? It's for you.'

Jimmy was lying on his bed watching Len Berman give the evening sports report. Former Celtic Don Nelson was in his first year of coaching the Knicks after Pat Riley had faxed his way to a better job with the Miami Heat. The future of the team was important. A call from a bill collector that he couldn't pay was less important. What was the point in answering the phone? The collector knew he wouldn't pay, but he had to make the call anyway. It was his job. It was his role in life to be a pain in the fucking ass.

Jimmy always got pissed off by the collectors' self-righteous attitudes. They were all such hypocrites. He had once read in a magazine that if you told a bill collector not to bother you any more and not to call you at home – he had to agree. If he called you again, he'd be breaking the law. In Jimmy's mind this was a more serious crime than his late payment of some bill. After all, it wasn't as if he was never going to pay the bill. Someday, when he had money, he'd be happy to pay whatever he owed. He just didn't have the cash at this particular time. A bill collector who called you after you told him he couldn't call you any more was deliberately committing criminal harassment. After Jimmy had shared this information with the last bill collector who had called him, the guy laughed and told him to fuck off. So what was the point of answering the hall phone right now? The guy on the other end was just as guilty of committing a crime as Jimmy was. Who the hell was he to give Jimmy shit? Fuck him. He stayed flat on his bed and shouted back to Girl 6, 'Tell 'em it's in the mail.'

Girl 6 didn't want any part of the phone call. 'Tell him yourself, man.'

Jimmy got out of bed and headed for the door. He was always happy to see Girl 6. He thought she was the best-looking woman in the New Amsterdam hotel. Probably the best-looking woman on the block, maybe even the whole godamn city. Who knows what might happen between them someday? A guy could have his dreams. Jimmy was not someone to let an opportunity pass without taking a shot.

Jimmy gave Girl 6 his best killer smile and picked up the phone. 'Jimmie no liva here, Jimmie no liva here.' Jimmy heard the bill collector shouting something about not giving him that spic bullshit as he slammed down the phone. Jimmy looked around. Girl 6 was gone. Damn. He had wanted her to see his performance. He thought it was pretty funny. He looked around and was pleased to see that Girl 6 had wandered into his room.

Girl 6 looked around Jimmy's room. If she was fascinated by her pantheon of women then Jimmy was equally obsessed with sports. The walls of the small room were covered with the back-cover sports pages of all the local newspapers. Many years ago Girl 6 had seen a movie called *The Omen*. In it, Gregory Peck and David Warner look for an obsessive character who knows a dark secret about Peck's baby son. When they found the guy's apartment they were stunned to see every inch of the room's walls covered with pages ripped from the bible. It was a pretty scary moment. Girl 6 looked at Jimmy's covered walls and thought of him as an obsessive high priest at the temple of sports. Jimmy could ignore his own lack of accomplishment by sublimating himself in the achievements of others. Like Girl 6, he had his dreams. He was sort of a hustler, too.

Girl 6 wanted to talk. 'How's business?' This was always a good subject with Jimmy. No matter how broke he was, there was always something that was about to break his way.

'It's kinda slow right now, but take a look at this. See this?' Jimmy showed Girl 6 a baseball card. 'In twenty years, this card will be worth a hundred times what it goes for now. I bought two thousand of them. Better than stocks.'

Girl 6 looked around Jimmy's cramped, cluttered room. She laughed. She couldn't help but like Jimmy's indomitable optimism. 'So all you gotta do is hold on for the next twenty years?'

Jimmy knew he liked Girl 6 for more than just her looks. She understood how he thought. She understood how things worked. 'Right, then I'll be a multimillionaire.'

Girl 6 giggled and thought about touching his cheek but didn't. Instead she asked, 'In the meantime . . .?'

Jimmy laughed too. He might have grandiose ambitions but he could also see exactly where he was right now. 'I'm a broke muthafucker.'

Now Girl 6 laughed out loud. 'Me and you both.'

Jimmy knew how to keep the conversation going. 'Any callbacks yet?'

The conversation from the hallway stretched into an afternoon in Girl 6's room. As always they eventually found themselves at Girl 6's vanity table. Girl 6 wanted to escape within someone else's glamor and Jimmy wanted to go along for the ride and be similarly transported. He noticed a picture of Girl 6 and her ex-husband from their wedding. The ex was good-looking and Jimmy didn't want any competition. He wanted to know if the coast was clear.

'You ever thought about getting back together?'

'No.' Girl 6 didn't care to elaborate. Her mind was already elsewhere. 'Close your eyes, Jimmy.'

Jimmy was ready to travel. He did as he was told. Girl 6 asked for her hair. Jimmy had the layout of Girl 6's vanity table memorized from many previous afternoons spent in her room. He handed Girl 6 her wig. She put it on. Girl 6 could feel herself changing. She was still in the room, however, and needed to talk about something she was worried about, something she was temporarily escaping from.

'Everybody's been okay so far. One of them's gotta call me, right? It's good money, too. I'm gonna get out of here. Four months max.' Maybe her next place wouldn't be Central Park West, but it would be someplace other than here.

Jimmy answered back, 'I'll tighten you up.'

Girl 6 just ignored him. 'It's good money if you're good. And I'm gonna be good. Eyes.'

Jimmy handed Girl 6 her fake eyelashes. 'Here. I's tighten you up.' Girl 6 put the eyelashes on and paid Jimmy no mind. Jimmy wouldn't shut up. 'If I were you, girl, I would hook up with your ex-man and have him rob me a bank.'

Girl 6 didn't laugh. 'Not funny. He stole my heart.'

Jimmy didn't like the sound of that. She still had feelings for her ex. Make her laugh. Make a joke about her ex's biggest failing.

'So steal it back.' Get the message, girl? Your ex is a fucking thief. Stay away from him. Stick around me; I don't have the same problem.

Girl 6 wasn't paying attention. 'Mouth.'

Jimmy handed her a lipstick. He still hadn't quite escaped his problems. 'Can I ask a favor?' he blurted out. Girl 6 nodded. Jimmy didn't want to be out on the street. 'I can't pay the rent.'

'Look,' she told him.

Jimmy opened his eyes. He recognized her immediately. 'Dorothy Dandridge.'

Girl 6 smiled. It was so easy. She wanted to help Jimmy – he had just helped her – but she couldn't.

'Jimmy, I ain't got it. Sell some of your autographs.'

Jimmy wasn't listening. He couldn't sell the memorabilia. They were his hope for the future.

He was persistent. 'You'll get it all back someday. I swear. Things will turn around.'

Girl 6 couldn't give him money she didn't have, so she changed the subject. 'A pretty good Dandridge, huh?'

Jimmy knew Dandridge was one of the most beautiful actresses in the history of film. For a moment he wasn't just a broke son of a bitch without much of a future. For a moment he was sitting next to, and having a conversation with, one of the most sensual women of the century. 'Hollywood's gonna eat you whole, girl.'

That would be just fine with Girl 6. 'Let's hope so,' she said.

Girl 6 was already somewhere else. Girl 6 was no longer Girl 6.

Girl 6 was now Dorothy Dandridge playing Carmen Jones in Otto Preminger's 1952 musical, *Carmen Jones*, based on Bizet's opera. Dandridge played the title role of the stunning temptress who leads Joe, a soldier and all-around good guy, to their mutual doom. In the movie Joe was played by a young Harry Belafonte, but in Girl 6's fantasy, the handsome shoplifter from the Korean deli played Belafonte playing Joe. Girl 6 replayed a scene that took place after Joe had killed his superior officer during a fight over Carmen. Escaping to Chicago the couple find themselves in a cheap south-side tenement that is constantly rattled by the passing El. At this point just being together is enough for the both of them. Their sexual pleasures transcend their poverty, but Joe begins to worry about Carmen's fidelity.

*Girl 6 as Dorothy Dandridge as Carmen sits in the dive in her bra and panties doing her toenails. The shoplifter as Harry Belafonte as Joe is eating a peach. Girl 6 as Dorothy Dandridge as Carmen offers the shoplifter as Harry Belafonte as Joe her toes. 'Blow on them honey.' Joe brings Girl 6's foot to his mouth and blows. Carmen coos, 'It makes them dry faster.' Joe becomes impassioned and begins to blow on Carmen's other foot. She's had enough. 'You can turn the heat off.' Carmen gets up and looks in her closet for a dress.*

*Joe begins to worry. 'You ain't going nowhere. You're staying here with me, where you belong.'*

*None of the 'three' women can accept this. 'Maybe you ain't got the message yet. Carmen is one girl nobody puts on a leash. No man is gonna tell me when I can come and go. I gotta be free or I don't stay at all.'*

*This sort of defiance really gets Joe going. He crosses the dingy room and grabs Girl 6. His voice is full of furious obsession. 'I'll follow you up to heaven or down to hell.'*

*Girl 6 grabs the peach from his hand and throws it across the room where it slams against the wall. Girl 6 and the shoplifter kiss like it's the last kiss of their lives. The camera of Girl 6's fantasy pans across the room and moves in for a close-up of the squashed piece of fruit as it clings to where it struck the wall. The music in her mind swells towards its flamboyant climax.*

# CHAPTER SEVEN

Girl 6 got the phone-sex job at the first place where she had interviewed. Her instincts had been right on target. Boss 1 had liked Girl 6 and hired her a few days after they met. Girl 6 arrived at the office for her first day of work wearing her auburn wig. She wasn't going to be quite herself, but she wasn't going to really be anyone else either – certainly none of the characters from the pictures on her wall.

Girl 6 walked up the two flights of stairs and was led into a room with six other new women awaiting their training session. Girl 6 was the most attractive of the new hires. The other women weren't exactly ugly, just more ordinary looking. Some looked sort of worn out. Some were plain. Others appeared a little strange. Girl 6 examined the other women carefully and was surprised to notice that the border between plainness and strangeness was surprisingly ambiguous. Her new co-workers could have been midwestern housewives or prison inmates. Maybe it was the flat lighting of the office and the fact that few of the women had bothered to dress up or wear makeup.

Girl 6 couldn't miss the photos of variously posed naked women hanging from the walls. They were probably there to create a positive atmosphere – to give the ordinary-looking phone-sex operators some inspiration, help them better see exactly what their ravishing fantasy characters might actually look like in the mind's eye of their callers. Girl 6 watched the way some of the women looked at the photos. Their eyes betrayed envy, awe and sometimes just disbelief. Girl 6 didn't care much either way.

Girl 6 smiled when Boss 1 entered the room looking like a teacher meeting her class at the beginning of a school year. Boss 1 introduced herself as 'Lil' and began her introductory lecture. Girl 6 listened for a while and then let her mind wander.

As Girl 6's eyes scanned the room's walls she saw something that made her laugh out loud. She had to turn her amusement into a staged cough so she didn't call too much attention to herself. Lil only paused for a moment and then continued. A few of the other women heard her and tried to see what was so funny. They saw the same thing but didn't see the humor. Girl 6 had noticed a number of 'distinguished service' plaques with a list of honored women's names listed beneath the elaborately filigreed pronouncement. Girl 6 had seen plenty of these inexpensive trophies growing up. You could get them almost anywhere for under ten bucks. They were a staple of a Queens kid's growing up and supposed to nurture ambition and reward achievement. If you went to a parochial school the sister might give a kid a trophy at the end of the year for 'most improvement' in math or bible study. Girl 6 had seen an award for most improved attitude at the home of her third-grade best friend, Nora Kelly. Her brother had received a plaque for being the funniest kid in his second-grade class. Girl 6 had even won her own award for 'actress most likely to succeed' after she played Juliet to Joe Ngyuen's Romeo in tenth grade. The idea of distinguishing yourself while performing phone sex struck Girl 6 as really funny. She was here for the cash. If the cash was good enough they could give the Academy Award to any of these other women. They looked like they needed something in their lives. Even winning attention as the most skilled phone-sex operator would be something worthwhile for them. Well, everyone could dream, couldn't they? That's exactly why they were here.

Girl 6 looked down at the handbook she had been given when she arrived. The woman at the desk had said a little too seriously that this was to be Girl 6's bible. She should learn it, love it – all that usual indoctrination bullshit. The manual had hot pink plastic covers and a swirling font that read, 900 FANTASY GIRL HANDBOOK. Inside, Girl 6 found chapters of photocopied instructions describing a variety of scenarios and characters that were suitable for performance. Girl 6 flipped through the pages quickly, but her attention went back to the florid sixties-style cover page. Something here interested her. Something bothered her. Something appealed to her. Girl 6 was slightly confused and didn't really know how she felt about what she saw. She wasn't even really sure what she was seeing. Instead of the various women's names, the covers had 'Girl #'s' printed in heavy Magic Marker.

The women who worked here didn't have names. They weren't the same people they had been when they walked out of their houses or apartments. As they traveled the streets or rode the subway to work their specific identities slipped away and were replaced by generic voids of personality – vacuums to be filled by that callers' fantasies. A young woman who had a perfectly good name, had grown up in a decent family, in a good neighborhood, had gone to school, led a life of her own with friends and personal interests – was eliminated and reborn as a repository for other people's desires. She was rechristened Girl 6.

The young woman sitting next to Girl 6, the daughter of an insurance salesman from Long Island, became Girl 19. Another woman from Chicago who needed money to pay her graduate school tuition became Girl 42. A woman who was a little hipper, a little punkish, a little East Village, became Girl 39. A middle-aged woman married to a cab driver became Girl 15. A woman in her late thirties who had just quit a corporate job to become a writer became Girl 21. A recently divorced woman with a high-school-aged son became Girl 3. A woman in her fifties who had several grandchildren that she adored became Girl 9.

Girl 6 thought about her new name only briefly. As an actress she had been so many names that it just didn't strike her as unusual at all. Girl 6 was no different from Juliet, Nina, Darlene, Rose, Maggie or Kitty. She would become Girl 6 while she was working in this office space and leave her behind when she went home after a shift. It was the same as becoming herself again after finishing a performance of *Hurly Burly, Cat on a Hot Tin*

*Roof*, or *Fences*. Maggie the Cat stayed behind in the theater and waited for the actress to return. She never got past the dressing rooms. Girl 6 would have to follow exactly the same rules – just the same as all the others, no big deal.

Girl 6's attention returned to Lil's talk. Lil was tapping a blackboard where she had printed a series of characters' names – basic roles that the phone-sex girls would assume. Girl 6 worked on creating identities for each of them – Bimbo, Nympho, TV, Mistress, Submissive and the Girl Next Door.

Lil was moving past the details and getting to the heart of the matter. '. . . because it's not just sex. You're their friend. They're lonely, they're divorced, their wives aren't into what they're into. They may be giants in the corporate world who are cross-dressers.' Lil really was an educator at heart. She stopped and took a look at her class to see who was and who wasn't paying attention.

'Girl 19, what's a crossdresser?' It was an absurdly simple question, she just wanted the girls to know that she expected them to be quick on their feet. That was part of the job.

Girl 19 fielded the inquiry easily. 'A man who likes women's clothes. For himself.'

Girl 4 had always liked school, although she hadn't gone past eleventh grade. She had always been a 'good girl', the type to sit at the front of the class, smile at the teacher, and shout out answers when her classmates were stumped. She didn't try to make them look stupid, but she did enjoy looking smarter. Most of her classmates thought she was sickening. Later on, they spent hours laughing when they learned that Girl 4 had gotten pregnant by the class clown and was never going to go to college. This wasn't quite college and it wasn't quite Mrs Berger's algebra class, but it was close enough. Girl 4 felt the thrill of knowing what the teacher wanted to hear. She got to show off how smart she was – something she hadn't been able to do in a long time.

'Or vice versa,' she said, pointing out that women were sometimes crossdressers too.

45

Lil looked at her a moment, surprised by her enthusiasm. Then she moved on – there were all types in this world.

'Crossdressers in their private lives, giants in the corporate world. You're the one who listens, you're the one who doesn't judge them. You want them to like you. 'Cause if they like you they call back and if they call back a lot . . .'

Girl 6 knew why she was there. 'You make the moolah.' Everyone laughed. They all thought they knew why they were there.

Lil had a lesson plan to stick to. She wanted her girls to have spirit and share a sense of camaraderie, but there was still business to attend to. 'Girl 19, run down your line-up.'

Girl 19, daughter of the Long Island insurance salesman, hesitated. She hadn't had a problem interviewing with Lil – that was one on one. She had spun some wild fantasies. Now, suddenly, she suffered exactly the same embarrassment she had always suffered from in school. Whenever a teacher called on her, Girl 19 had turned totally red and started to sweat. Why did she have to go first? She would have been a whole lot more comfortable if someone else had gone first. Lil wasn't feeling especially patient. She didn't like it when she made mistakes in hiring. Mistakes wasted time. Time was money. They charged by the minute.

'Girl 19, you are in the wrong business to be shy.'

Girl 19 pulled herself together and ran down her roster of fantasy characters. 'My bimbo is Stacey. Thirty-eight double D, twenty-five, thirty-eight. Sandy blond hair. Blue eyes like the deep blue sea. Never finished high school.'

Lil didn't care if Stacey the Bimbo hadn't finished high school or if she'd gotten a doctorate in advanced neurophysiology and performed brain surgery daily at Columbia Presbyterian. Background was unimportant. Could Stacey the Bimbo perform when it came to selling sex? That was all that counted. 'All right, Girl 19. Everyone's going to close their eyes. Let's hear you pick up the phone as Stacey.'

Girl 19 figured it was best to just dive in. She nervously began her sexy, Stacey the Bimbo voice. 'Hi, my name's Stacey. What's your name?'

Lil cut her off, there was no point in wasting everybody's time. 'Whadoyathink, girls?' No one was impressed. On the Bimbometer, Stacey flopped. Girl 6 knew she'd do a much better job when she was called. Girl 19's effort had been weak. Lil's sternness dissipated, surprising everyone. If she had made a mistake in hiring Girl 19, she wasn't ready to accept failure so soon. Lil spoke like a friendly coach, trying to teach but also instill confidence.

'Try Stacey again. Come on, toss that blond hair and pinch your double D's. If that's what it takes to get you to Stacey-land, do it and let's hear it.'

Girl 19 rode the wave of Lil's generous spirit and took another shot. Her words weren't particularly memorable – 'Hi, my name's Stacey. What's yours?' – but her new voice was. Girl 6 looked at Girl 19 with some surprise. Wow. Girl 19 did have it after all, didn't she?

Lil was pleased with Girl 19's progress. 'Let's hear your Nympho.'

Girl 19 had a little more confidence this time. 'My Nympho's name is Linda.'

Lil had to interrupt, 'Sorry, Linda is taken, try another.'

Girl 19 offered up, 'Brenda.'

Lil was happy to see that Girl 19 was could think fast. 'Brenda is free.'

Girl 19 was on a roll, 'Nympho: Brenda. Jet black hair, thirty-eight Cs, silver-dollar nipples. Five-feet, four-inches tall. Humps whatever walks.'

The class felt good about Girl 19's success. As their nervousness faded a team spirit grew between them. Girl 12 loved what she was hearing. She couldn't help but shout out, 'Walk the walk, talk the talk!'

Lil felt the class was going to be just fine. She only had to lay

47

down a few more ground rules. 'Brenda can do anything but animals. That's one of the No's. Here's the No list. Take notes.'

Girl 6 watched as some of the others began to write in the margins of their fantasy girl handbooks. Lil went down the list, 'No violent rapes, no incest, no under eighteens – either you or the caller, no mutilation, no bestiality. Just tell them politely, "Sorry honey I'm not allowed to do that with you." If they insist hand them over to a supervisor. Okay? Girl 6, who's your TV girl?'

Girl 6 didn't hesitate. She had done exercises like this for years. It was just a new kind of improv. 'Esmerelda. Whopper couchie. Ready to please. Jet black hair. Hot green eyes. Pre-op.' Lil and the others liked what they heard. Girl 6 continued on, not waiting for any prompting from Lil. 'My Mistress – I haven't figured her out yet. Maybe "April" . . . My Girl Next Door's name is gonna be "Lovely."'

Girl 12 was surprised. 'Lovely?'

Girl 6 was proud of her creation, 'Yeah. Lovely Brown.'

Girl 19, flush from her own victory, wanted to congratulate Girl 6 on hers. 'That's cute.'

Lil knew she had hired a terrific group. She could see their sisterly camaraderie growing already. That was good for business. She wanted to know if Girl 6 could find a voice equal to fulfill the potential of a name like 'Lovely Brown.' Lil turned to Girl 6. 'Let's see if it fits.'

Girl 6 slipped into her sexiest Girl Next Door persona. 'Ooooh. Hey there. My name's Lovely. What's yours?' The roomful of women cheered.

Lil wanted to hear more. 'Take her to the bank, Girl 6. What's Lovely like?'

Girl 6 knew exactly what Lovely Brown was like. 'Dark hair, dark eyes. Hot but shy. Kinda freaky.'

Lil thought the group was ready to proceed to the next level. 'Good. Unless a caller requests, all your girls are w-h-i-t-e. Additional characters can include Black girls, Puerto Rican girls,

Asian girls, the whole ethnic gambit, also foreign girls – English and French accents, etcetera. Read up on your current events. Especially the sports. How about those Knicks! Okay? So far so good.' Lil looked at a computer monitor in front of her. 'Great, another call's coming in on line seventeen. The monitor tells us it's a domination fantasy. Plug in, pick up and listen.'

Girl 6 looked at the monitor in front of her and the elaborate phone system. She and the other women plugged themselves in. Lil looked at them with satisfaction. They looked to her like a well-drilled unit of army recruits.

# CHAPTER EIGHT

A few nights later, Girl 6 pulled her first shift. Arriving a half hour before she was to take her calls, Girl 6 noticed that the other women were all in casual clothing. She was dressed in an outfit that was reminiscent of Marilyn Monroe's in the picture on her apartment wall. Girl 6 was also wearing her black bobbed wig and elaborate fingernails. She knew she was overdressed but that was okay with her. Costumes were part of any role and were important for performance. They also provided the added benefit of protection. Wearing Marilyn's dress, Girl 6 was already in an alternate character even before she began spinning fantasies for callers.

Girl 6 looked for the cubicle that she had been assigned the other day. She was one of twenty and had entered the wrong cubicle at first because all of the pre-fabricated units looked exactly alike. Girl 11 showed her to the right place. Now Girl 6 was only moments away from beginning her new job. Keeping one hand on the telephone receiver, her phone jack in the other, Girl 6 stared at her computer monitor waiting for things to start. Girl 6 looked at the empty pages of her log book and wondered how long it would take her to fill them. How many pages would it be before she had enough money to quit and move to Hollywood? Her eyes moved over the desk to a set of index cards she had covered in her neat handwriting. One card was a detailed description of Lovely Brown – her Girl Next Door. A second card provided detail on her TV character, Esmerelda. Girl 6 hadn't figured out who her Bimbo was yet but thought she could do that tonight during down time. Girl 6's mouth was a little dry with nervousness. She opened a can of Dr Pepper and stuck in a straw. Girl 6 was ready for action, but nothing was happening.

Girl 6 looked around her spartan cubicle trying to keep her mind focused on the evening's activities. Someone had distributed Lil's list of forbidden fantasies. Girl 6 pulled out a piece of paper from her handbook and taped it to a wall – the page showed a chart that would help Girl 6 calculate the age of her callers. She put it up but didn't figure she'd need to use it. Girl 6 could figure out how old a guy was in her head, but taping the chart was something to do. Not much, but something. There. It was up. She had done something. She had a sense of accomplishment. She had already done something that night. Bullshit. She had no sense of accomplishment. Girl 6 just had a case of nerves. She wished she could get started. This was how it had always been for her. Waiting to go on stage, she'd be frightened, but once she stepped into character she would always relax and do fine. Girl 6 pulled another page from her handbook and hung it up. She looked it over. The page listed a set of pointers under the heading, 'How to keep him interested.' Another page listed a post-office box with instructions that described what to do if 'a caller wants to write to you.' Another page showed a crude schematic on how to entertain 'Two at once.' The following, more ambitious page, instructed Girl 6 in how to handle 'Four at once.' Under each drawing was a concise and not terribly convincing encouragement: 'You can do it!'

A red button flashed on Girl 6's telephone. Adrenalin coursed through her body. This was it. Showtime. Take a deep breath. Center. Focus. No problem. She was ready for anything. Girl 6 checked out the monitor, read the telephone line number of the incoming call, and plugged herself in quickly. She offered a 'Hello!' that sounded like she was trying too hard. She knew it was phoney as soon as it left her mouth. She'd have to do better than that. Fuck.

But it wasn't a problem. The person on line seven wasn't a caller but Salesgirl 1. 'It's just me. Something'll come up in a minute. We're gonna start you off slow. Nothing too wild. First call is like a first date. We'll send you someone fabulous.'

51

Salesgirl 1 wanted to calm Girl 6 down. 'Nothing too wild. Just be yourself.'

Girl 19 walked by Girl 6's cubicle wearing a corsage. She leaned over and gave Girl 6 a kiss on the cheek. 'You're gonna be great.' She walked away leaving Girl 6 alone with her nerves.

A call came in. Girl 6 read her monitor and plugged herself into line fifteen. For a moment she didn't say anything. Should she let the caller say hello first? Would that put him in control of the situation? Would that make him happier? She didn't know which role he wanted her to play. Which character should answer the phone?

Caller 3 wasn't accustomed to silence. 'Hello. Hello? Anybody home?'

Girl 19 was walking by again and saw Girl 6 freeze up. 'Go ahead, that's money talking, girl.'

Girl 6 shook off her fear. She would take it as it came. 'Hi there. How are you tonight?' Caller 3 was happy his connection fee hadn't been wasted.

'Horny. I thought I had lost you. I'm Steve.'

He was insecure, afraid of rejection, maybe even abandonment. Or was Girl 6 thinking about things too much, screwing herself up – maybe that was just all in her head. Relax. Take things as they came. Be yourself. Yeah, right. Girl 6 made a mental note and ran with it. 'I'm right here baby.' She would provide the comforting he craved. 'Where ya calling from?' He was calling from Houston. 'You're in Texas? It's hot down there, huh?'

Caller 3 agreed. 'Hot and sticky . . . what's your name?'

Girl 6 sized up Caller 3 and figured him for a Girl Next Door type. 'I'm Lovely. Lovely Brown. Let me tell you about myself. I got dark eyes, dark hair. I got a figure to die for.'

Caller 3 was hooked. 'And you got big ones, dontcha?'

Lovely Brown did have big ones. 'Thirty-eight D – double Ds. Nice, big, firm and healthy.'

Girl 6 looked up and saw Girl 19 watching. Girl 19 offered a big grin and flashed a thumbs-up. Girl 6 was going to be fine.

Caller 3 wanted more. 'Don't be fibbing now. I was hoping you had 'em. Love them big teets. Big like Texas.'

By now Girl 6 knew the theme he wanted to hear and began her variations of his melody. 'Silver-dollar nipples. Really sensitive. Twenty-five-inch waist, thirty-five-inch hips. And yeah, I'm a deep throat, Stephen.' A little sweat had broken out on Girl 6's face, but she didn't notice it. Girl 6 was totally focused on the call and her goal of providing Caller 3 with satisfaction. Five minutes earlier Girl 6 would have told you that doing this sort of work meant nothing but a paycheck. Now, before the end of her first call, Girl 6 was already losing her sense of self – she was inside Lovely Brown – and making Caller 3 come was all that mattered.

Caller 3 was on his way. 'You know what I did today? I made a million dollars.'

Lovely Brown wasn't skeptical. No way. Caller 3 said he had a million dollars so surely he had. 'Really? Howdja do that?'

Caller 3 told his story. 'Bought a little. Sold a lot.'

In the salesroom, Lil sat at her desk and listened in on Girl 6's call. Salesgirl 1 came over and asked, 'How's she doing?'

Lil was pleased with Girl 6 already. 'Started out shaky, but she'll be all right.' Lil continued to listen in on Girl 6's conversation and watched as Girl 29 strolled into the salesroom.

Caller 3 was explaining to Girl 6 how the system worked. 'Company A is a hammer. Company B is something pricey. A diamond, say. Say a big hard pricey rock. Get me?'

Girl 6 threw a little awe into her voice. 'Gotcha.'

Girl 29 picked up a telephone, signed it out, and signed on for the night. Lil asked her for her number. Girl 29 smiled, juggled the phone and her log sheet and flashed twenty-nine fingers. Lil made a note.

'I use company A to smash company B,' Caller 3 continued. 'I sell all the little diamond chips at a jacked-up price.'

Girl 6 moaned appreciatively.

Caller 3 liked that. 'And *voilà*. A million dineros.'

Girl 6 was doing a good job of making Caller 3 feel like a million dineros. 'I'm getting excited just thinking about it.' Girl 6 was taking Caller 3 where he wanted to go. Focused as she was, Girl 6 didn't even notice Ronnie the security guard as he walked by carrying hot take-out Chinese.

Caller 3 figured he had spent enough time charming Girl 6 and could now get down to the real matter at hand. 'I bet I could hump you any time I wanted to, couldn't I?'

Girl 6 was now in the business of agreeing. She chose response 3 from the fantasy girl's handbook. 'Yes. I'm horny all the time so I'd really like it.'

Caller 3 figured she would and fell silent while he contemplated the possibilities. Girl 6 didn't want the conversation to lag; she wanted to keep Caller 3 on the line. The job was all about minutes. 'Are you single?'

Caller 3 was married.

'Does your wife know you're calling me?'

'Nope. You single?'

Girl 6 was. Caller 3 suddenly missed his single days. 'So you can do whatever you want? I'm jealous.'

Girl 6 knew exactly what he wanted to hear. 'I do whatever *you* want, baby.'

Caller 3 was left speechless with expectation. Girl 6 knew she had him where she wanted him.

'Are you good and hard for me, Stephen?' Caller 3 was good and hard for her.

Before Girl 6 could close the deal, Ronnie, the Chinese-food-bearing security guard, shouted that dinner was ready. In the sales office, Lil told Ronnie to be quiet. 'Shhh. Get me a flower.' Ronnie knew that somewhere out there in the great expanse that was America, some lonely guy was about to come by himself while accompanied by the voice of one of the ladies in the next room. He shrugged and went to do as he was told. Ronnie was more interested in the Strange Flavored Beef and Kung Pao Chicken than some loser asshole stroking his own won-tons.

Girl 6 concentrated and asked Caller 3, 'Are you wet up top?'

Caller 3 was. 'Yeah. Sit on my lap and jiggle for me.'

Girl 6 did as she was told. 'Okay. I'm wearing a light white T-shirt and a little skirt . . .'

Caller 3 was racing down the home stretch. He couldn't even wait to the end of her description. 'Jiggle for me, Lovely. Bounce 'em up and down.'

Girl 6 breathed quickly as though from some form of exertion. 'I'm bouncing. I'm on your lap and my big tits are bouncing up and down for you, Stevic.'

That did it. Somewhere in Texas, Caller 3 struck oil. 'Ooooh. Yeah – Hhhh. Thanks, honey.'

He hung up without saying anything more and Girl 6 was left with the dial tone.

The dial tone was only momentary. Salesgirl 1 had been monitoring the call from the sales office and shouted to Girl 6, 'Congratulations!!' Girl 6 was beside herself. She couldn't believe she had made a guy come over the phone just by talking to him. Wow. That was some power.

'The guy came! His name is Steve. I hope I did good.' Girl 6 had done good and Lil entered her cubicle carrying a corsage in a plastic box that Ronnie had just taken out of the refrigerator.

'He hung up happy. Good job. How do you feel?' Girl 6 felt okay. Her mouth was a little dry. Lil understood. 'Drink your soda. Good. This is for you. You broke your cherry.' Lil proudly pinned the corsage to Girl 6's dress. Girl 6 shivered from the flower's cold.

# CHAPTER NINE

Girl 6 had been on the job for about two weeks. Her cubicle now had some identifying clutter, but not too much. She had to share it with two other women. Girl 6 sat at her station, wearing an auburn wig. She was still overdressed for the job. Girl 6 was reviewing her file of characters and callers when the computer screen flashed a request. Girl 6 checked to see what she would be. The Caller wanted a blond housewife fantasy. Girl 6 flipped through her cards and found the right character. She plugged in her phone and picked up. 'Hey there. I'm so glad you called.'

Caller 4 wasn't interested in small talk. 'I'm calling from my beach house, housewife. Let's start in the kitchen, there's whipped cream in the refrigerator.'

Caller 4's feet played in the sand as he sat on the beach. The sky was a stunning, shocking blue in Florida. The afternoon rain shower had cleared the beach for a while. Caller 4 sat alone with the waves and the seagulls.

He smiled and tensed a little when Girl 6 began her conversation. 'Ooooh. I've been on my feet all day and now I'm on my hands and knees cleaning the kitchen floor. I'd love to take a break and talk with you.'

Caller 4 liked his women on the floor doing demeaning work. 'You're scrubbing the floor? Good. Keep scrubbing, if you don't mind. We can talk while you work.'

Girl 6 sat in her cubicle. Maybe Caller 4 liked his women in subservient positions. Or maybe he was just a neatness freak and wanted her to finish what she had started. It didn't matter. Either way, Girl 6 worked towards the same goal.

While Girl 6 talked with Florida, some of her co-workers took a break. There were overstuffed chairs, a ragged couch, a coffee machine and a refrigerator filled with junk food in the undecorated lounge. It was late and Girl 39, Girl 4 and Girl 58 sat around drinking stale supermarket coffee and eating chips. Girl 19 tried to have a private conversation with her boyfriend on a payphone. Girl 19 hoped her boyfriend couldn't hear what her friends were talking about. He had an open mind, but really only regarding the things he did. Girl 19 wasn't so sure he could handle the true nature of her work. She had told him that she was in telephone sales – suggesting something about long-distance services and joking about 'reaching out and touching someone.' Well, in its own way it was true.

Girl 39 had an irreverent sense of humor. She loved her job. It paid well and she saw the whole thing as a big joke. Well, maybe it was more than just a joke. It appealed to her feminist principles in a perversely ironic sort of way – making good cash by taking money off a group of horny, misogynistic pricks. She didn't share her feelings with the others and some of them wondered just why she always seemed to be laughing. Girl 39 had moved to New York years ago without any specific purpose. She had grown up in Detroit and all she knew was that she wanted out of her home town – fast. Heading to the Greyhound station one day she realized she had enough money for Manhattan but not Los Angeles. The choice had been made for her.

Girl 39 had a great time telling the others about her last call. 'I made him do the sounds of each and every barnyard animal before he fucked them – and he did it too. No shit.'

Girl 58 hummed a few bars from a nursery school song and then asked, 'What was he, like, the Farmer-in-the-Dell?'

Everyone laughed and Girl 39 ran with the joke. 'The fucking Farmer-in-the-Deli.' When she caught her breath again, Girl 39 replayed the highlights from the call. 'You waana hump that cow, slave? Lemme hear the cow-sound and Mistress Tina will let you hump the cow, slave – an' he goes MOOOO! MMM-MOOOOO!! He really did. No shit.'

Girl 19 tried to cover the sound of the shouting and laughter with her body. There was no way she could offer an explanation for the mooing cow so she didn't bother to try. Fortunately, her boyfriend was exhausted from a long day fixing cars. If he even heard the cow, somehow it hadn't registered in his mind. Girl 19 didn't give him much of a chance to think about it though and moved right along with the conversation. 'Honey, you don't have to pick me up. I can get home fine. Seven a.m. it's light out, I'll be fine. Subscriptions. For magazines, yeah.' The other day the boyfriend had wanted to show he supported Girl 19's career and offered to switch over from Sprint. Girl 19 had quickly told him that her division had been bought by Publisher's Clearing House and that she might be selling subscriptions soon. She was good at making up stories – it's how she earned her living. Maybe now was a good time to hear that damn cow again. It'd be an easier question to answer.

Girl 39 went on with the details of the Farmer-in-the-Deli. 'And after he finished fucking Bossy.'

Girl 4 had to interrupt, 'He had names for 'em?'

No he hadn't. Girl 39 had to supply the fictional animals' names too. 'I had names for 'em. He finished with Bossy and he's ready for Freddy. Ladies, Freddy is the pig.'

Girl 4 had to correct her, 'Arnold is the pig.'

Girl 19 wanted to hear from the pig, the cow – any barnyard animal would do. The boyfriend needed some sort of distraction. Girl 19 thought he was sweet but an increasing pain in the ass. He was still earnestly trying to help. If he couldn't change phone services, he'd buy magazine subscriptions – if it would help her. What magazines did she sell? Girl 19 prayed for some sort of divine intervention and rattled off a few respectable names, '*Time. Newsweek.* Jesus. *Cosmo.*'

Girl 39 finished her story with a rousing imitation of her beast-loving caller, 'OINK! OINK! OINK! OINK!'

Girl 19 figured it was best to quit while she was ahead, rattled the telephone's button, claimed the connection was going bad, and hung up.

Girl 6 was still spinning the blond housewife fantasy. Caller 4

58

was a good customer – the minutes were adding up. In the cubicle next to her, Girl 42 was weaving a supermarket fantasy with Caller 16. As she sexed him, Girl 42 did her trigonometry homework. Girl 6 had no distractions. She stared straight ahead and concentrated.

Girl 42 had gone shopping, 'with no bra on. You know, go grocery shopping at the A&P like that.' Caller 16 didn't have much of a sense of humor and went for the obvious joke trying to impress Girl 42.

'I'd be the stock boy and grab your melons.' He shouldn't have bothered. Girl 42 had heard the line many times before.

'Yesterday I went grocery shopping,' she continued.

Caller 16 interrupted again. 'Whatdidja buy?'

That was fine with Girl 42. It just meant he'd be on her phone that much longer. She answered his question. 'Soup, asparagus, oyster crackers, you know, for the soup.' It wasn't the most exciting answer, but her mind was on her math problem and Caller 16 didn't seem to be too demanding.

Girl 6 kept Caller 4 on the phone. 'I'm making slow, soapy circles on the linoleum with my scrub brush.'

'What color's the linoleum?' Caller 4 liked details.

What difference did it make? What the hell, it was his fantasy. 'Yellow.'

Caller 4 thought yellow was perfect. Sitting in his deck-chair at the beach, he watched the waves. Behind him, a child built an elaborate sandcastle.

Caller 4 listened, mesmerized, to Girl 6. 'Yellow with little daisies. Slow, soapy circles on my hands and knees.'

Caller 4 wanted to know where his blond housewife's kids were. They were taking naps. Good. Caller 4 hated it when kids interfered with his romantic liaisons. Caller 4 was ready for some serious sex.

'I'm pushing your dress up above your hips. I'm going to mount you doggie style.' Girl 6 offered an appreciative moan.

Caller 4 had more instructions. 'Don't stop scrubbing. I'm

mounting you, housewife. You got so much work to do. Don't stop scrubbing. Don't stop scrubbing. A woman's work is never done.'

The morning arrived fairly quickly. Girl 6 had done well that night and was feeling good. Girl 6 and Girl 39 walked home. The sun was up but most of the city's commuters were still in the shower or having breakfast. Girl 39 wanted to know how Girl 6 was doing. Girl 6 had big news to share.

'I got my first request tonight!'

Girl 39 was pleased for her but also had some advice. She had been watching Girl 6's technique and was a little worried.

'Do something while you talk. Read a magazine or something. Don't just sit there, or you can get hooked.'

Girl 6 didn't think she would be able to do that. She was still new to the business. 'I'm concentrating.' Girl 6 didn't like the idea of doing something else while she worked. It might be fine for the other women, but Girl 6 wanted to be the best at what she did. If you didn't pay attention then you weren't doing the best job possible. If you weren't doing the best job possible then you were losing time and money with your callers. Girl 6 wanted to earn more money than anyone else. That's all. That's what she was about. That's why she was there. The more she made, the sooner she could leave.

Girl 39 wasn't convinced by Girl 6's answer. She tried to make her point again. '*Do* something. Okay?'

Girl 6 was getting tired of the conversation. She was sullen, almost insulted when she agreed, 'Yeah.'

To Girl 39, this was a bad sign. Girl 6 was being too defensive – maybe she was starting to have a problem. Girl 39 figured this was no time for diplomacy. Straight talk was required.

'You don't come with 'em, do ya?'

Girl 6 rolled her eyes, too tired to get angry.

'Please.' Her tone suggested that nothing could be further from the truth.

Girl 39 reached her street and looked Girl 6 over. She wasn't convinced Girl 6 knew what she was getting into, but she had said all she was going to say on the matter. She had offered good advice. Now, it was up to Girl 6 to take it or leave it.

Girl 39 said goodnight. 'This is me. Later.' She crossed the street to her apartment.

Girl 6 watched her go. She appreciated the big-sisterly concern but thought that Girl 39 was out of line. She was an adult. She was in control of herself. She was in control of the situation.

Girl 6 continued uptown and eventually reached her neighborhood. Still several blocks from the New Amsterdam Royal, Girl 6 spotted a Russian fruit vendor. The produce looked pretty good, but she decided to be loyal to the market on her street. As she passed, Girl 6 spotted the shoplifter, once again catching him in the act. She tried not to look but found her eyes drawn back to him. Even half a block up the street, Girl 6 turned around to see what he was doing. The shoplifter made eye contact and smiled warmly. Girl 6 turned around and walked home all the faster.

# CHAPTER TEN

Girl 6 had cooked dinner for Jimmy. She opened the toaster oven and pulled out two TV dinners. She ripped back the tops of the containers and steam poured out. Girl 6 and Jimmy were having pot roast in gravy with roasted potatoes and vegetables. Jimmy unscrewed the top of a sensibly economical gallon of decent Californian wine. He poured two glasses. He had something on his mind.

'One month down, only three more to go, right? How long you gonna do this phone stuff?'

Girl 6 emptied the dinners carefully on to two plates, trying to keep the food separated. 'Who knows. I'm starting to like it. My endurance is improving and I'm real popular.'

Lil had told her only last night that she had never seen some-one become so popular so quickly. Girl 6 was closing in on a 900-number record.

'I had thirty-eight calls last night. Seventeen requests. That's like almost 50 per cent, right?'

Jimmy didn't like what he heard. Who did she think she was, an X-rated Sally Field? They like her. They liked her. So fucking what? This wasn't a job for a girl like her. But Jimmy kept his mouth shut. He knew he couldn't tell Girl 6 what to do. If she was going to realize anything she would have to realize it on her own.

They had pretty much finished their meal and were sitting on Girl 6's bed. She flipped through her caller log – a bunch of index cards in a recipe file box. Girl 6 pulled a man's card out and told Jimmy all about him.

'He needed me real bad. I was Mistress April. The guy loved pain. Wanted me to keep count as he pulled his pubic hairs out one by one with tweezers.'

Jimmy practically fell off the bed he was laughing so hard. 'I can see that! Ow! – one. Oww! – two. Owwww! – three. Owwwww! – four.'

Girl 6 was pleased by the memory of the caller. 'He got off. And I got good minutes on him too. Plus three requests. 'Cos he called back three times. He needed it bad. He was calling from his penthouse.'

Jimmy didn't believe the penthouse bit and looked at her with disbelief. Girl 6 wanted him to know she was telling the truth.

'They pay with credit cards so we have their addresses. I had this pilot call. Cockpit fuck fantasy at twenty-five-thousand feet with Brigitte, the busty blonde. Suck – ah!' Brigitte was Girl 6's bimbo. She had finally come up with a name.

Jimmy wasn't any less skeptical than he was before. 'A pilot called you? No wonder those planes been falling out of the sky left and right.' Girl 6 imagined the pilot talking down the nervous passengers after he got off. She could hear the lazy cowboy drawl apologizing for the unexpected turbulence that occurred when he beat off to the sounds of Bimbo Brigitte's affectionate attention. Of course, maybe he wasn't an airline pilot. How could he have whacked off with the co-pilot sitting next to him? On the other hand, maybe the co-pilot had gotten off for free – a two-for-one. That would have been a violation of the FAA laws, wouldn't it?

Girl 6 offered Jimmy some more wine. He declined. Girl 6 poured him a glass anyway and pulled out another card from her file.

'Bobby from Tucson, my first steady regular. Fastest comer in the west. He babbles about his mom.'

Jimmy had heard enough. He didn't find the subject as interesting as Girl 6 did, and besides, he didn't like the idea of a girl like her doing shit work like she did. He thought she was moving in the wrong direction.

'Any good auditions lately?'

Girl 6 didn't even hear Jimmy's question. She was too

wrapped up in Bobby from Tucson's mother. 'Something about her dying or something and he doesn't wanna visit 'cause they don't get along and . . .'

Jimmy was pissed off. He didn't give a shit about Bobby from Tucson, masturbating airplane pilots, or Girl 6's various fantasy characters. He gave a shit about Girl 6 though.

'What happened to your acting career?'

'I'm still an actor,' Girl 6 answered immediately.

That got Jimmy angrier. 'Not the kind I know. This isn't the move!'

Girl 6 was pretty adept with talking guys down nowadays. Jimmy was no different. She didn't back down. 'Jimmy baby, you can keep living in a fantasy world if you want to with that baseball-card bullshit. I gotta eat and pay my rent. Phone sex is acting. You don't like it – step.' Jimmy got up and shook his head as he left.

When Jimmy had shut the door, Girl 6 sighed with relief. She had to spend all her working days telling guys what they wanted to hear. She was beat and didn't want to have to do it in her own home on her own time. If Jimmy wanted to lecture somebody about what was what, he ought to start with himself. He wasn't in much of a position to tell anybody what to do. Girl 6 didn't want to talk with anybody else, not right now, not even if she got paid. She wanted someone to tell *her* something for a change. It didn't matter what. Girl 6 turned on the television.

Two attractive newscasters with the personality of margarine wore their 'sad story' faces. The news they were broadcasting was tragic and they wanted to make sure their audience understood that. In hushed tones and with her jaw set, Newscaster Carol Young told a grim story. 'In Harlem tonight there is tragedy. After-school play has turned into a most deadly game. Nita Hicks is live at the scene. Nita?'

Reporter Nita Hicks stood outside a large apartment building on Lennox Avenue, not all that far away from Girl 6's home. Nita had a good story and she knew it would get her terrific exposure.

Tens of thousands of viewers would see her telling this story. She would be identified with the awful events. She would stick with the story, canceling all other commitments so that she and the story would be irrevocably linked. This wasn't a vapid human-interest story about twins separated at birth who were being re-united after sixty-five years. This was a real news story and Nita had a hard time keeping the excitement out of her voice when she told the tale.

'Carol. It started out as an after-school game between two little girls. In the high-rise apartment building in back of me here on 125th Street and Lennox Avenue, the game played between two little girls has played out into a family's worst nightmare.'

This story could get Nita national offers. She remembered the kid who fell down the well and got stuck. It was down south, about ten years ago. Audiences were glued to their sets watching events unfold minute by minute. They couldn't get enough. The local reporter – some badly dressed desert rat from Horse Shit, Texas – had gone to CNN after that, or at least that's how Nita remembered it. This story could be her ticket out.

The news report cut to an interior shot of a badly maintained apartment building lobby. An elevator door with yellow police tape across it became the focus of the shot. Nita spoke with great sadness over the imagery.

'It was in this hallway, at this door, that the girls' game of tag led to tragedy.' A grade-school photograph of a cute, bright little girl was flashed on the screen. The girl wore a Catholic school uniform. 'Witnesses say eight-year-old Angela King was running down the sixth floor hallway when she leaned against the elevator door.' Angela's photograph was replaced by footage of the dingy hallway and the taped-over door. 'The elevator was not on the sixth floor but up on the eighteenth floor and the elevator door should have been secure. The door was not secure – it gave way and . . .' The report cut to home-video footage of an adorable Angela smiling into the camera, '. . . eight-year-old Angela King fell through the empty elevator shaft, falling six floors down into the basement.'

The report cut to Angela's parents' apartment. Nita stood next to a tearful middle-aged woman, Angela's aunt. Nita put a consoling arm around the aunt's shoulders and spoke into the camera. 'She was rushed to Harlem Hospital and they tell me she has now been transferred to Mount Sinai where she suffers from multiple skull fractures. She is in intensive care and in critical condition.'

Girl 6 watched the report. Her face was calm and relaxed. Angela's grieving aunt spoke her grief.

'I'm Angela's aunt. I dunno. Her mama's up at the hospital with her right now. I just done. Her daddy's still at work. What's he gonna say when he comes home?' Girl 6's face remained impassive.

That night Girl 6 dreamed. In her dream she walked through the hallways of Angela's dilapidated apartment building. The elevator doors opened for her. She walked through – but there was no elevator there to keep her from falling. Girl 6 looked down – the pitch black shaft seemed to go down an infinite distance. Girl 6 started to fall.

## CHAPTER ELEVEN

Girl 6 sat at her station working the phone. As usual, she stared straight ahead at some unseen point on the cubicle wall. She was concentrating, lost within and riveted by the caller's fantasy. Her eyes looked at – but didn't see – a newspaper article about little Angela King's fall. It was taped on the wall next to one of Lil's encouraging platitudes: 'You can do it!' Caller 7 was sharing some personal information about himself with Girl 6. 'I'm the world's greatest stockbroker. I make money hand over fist. I got five Ferraris, one for Monday through Friday. I'm the man. You want a Rolex, I'll buy you a Rolex, just make me come. I don't come easy, that's worth a Rolex.'

Girl 6 was momentarily distracted. Shit. If she had a Rolex for every guy she made come, she'd have her own fucking jewelry business by now.

In an adjacent cubicle Girl 19 talked with Callers 8, a husband and wife called Martin and Christine. Girl 19 had been enlisted as something of an X-rated therapist named Sheila.

'Christine, maybe you should take me off speaker phone and you and me could talk about Martin. You know, woman to woman.'

Christine wasn't sure; she had a tough time making up her own mind.

Martin wasn't so indecisive. 'Sheila, why don't you just tell my ice-cold wife what she can do to please me.'

As Christine protested that she wasn't ice-cold, Girl 19 leaned over her cubicle partition and made a 'this is so boring' face to Girl 6. Girl 6 gave a quick understanding grin and returned her attentions to Caller 7.

Somewhere in Washington DC a man sat in the living room of his high-rise apartment building. Looking through a large picture window he could see all of the nation's greatest monuments beneath him – the Lincoln and Jefferson memorials, the Capitol building, the White House, the Washington Monument. Caller 9 was sitting in his chair, twenty-five stories above the city, looking down on all of it. Caller 9 told Girl 39 that his name was Ingmar, but that was bullshit. He might have been any number of powerful men in town – maybe diplomatic, maybe press, maybe money, maybe even a suddenly powerful conservative politician. Girl 39 thought she detected a slight southern twang but couldn't be sure. 'Do you have any restrictions? Anything you don't like, Ingmar?' Ingmar had no restrictions. 'So tell Mistress Tina your favorite things.'

Caller 9 ran a hand through his salt and pepper hair, down his slightly pudgy stomach and on to a table where an assortment of 'toys' waited for him.

'Mistress Tina. I like to be dominated.' His hand fondled a nipple clip, a tube of Ben Gay. Girl 39 responded calmly, coolly, knowingly, as though there were nothing at all unusual in his request, which in fact there wasn't.

'We know that, Ingmar.'

Caller 9 shuddered as he touched a pair of pantyhose, a neatly coiled clothesline, and rested his hands on a small dildo. 'I like to be dominated by Black women, Mistress Tina.'

A few hundred miles away in Manhattan, Girl 39 quickly swallowed a bite of her burrito and washed it down with some herbal tea. Girl 39 added to her file on Caller 9. She wrote, 'Black women!' on to an index card. A fragment of bean got caught in her throat and she took another quick gulp of tea to wash it away. Caller 9 was excited by the pause – his sense of anticipation grew. Girl 39 flipped through her file, found the card on her Black dominatrix character, and went to work.

'That's why they sent you to me, honey. What else do you like, Ingmar?' Caller 9 liked to be smothered. He liked ass worship.

Caller 9 was thrilled to hear that Girl 39 had a really big ass. He compulsively rearranged his toys and breathed a little more rapidly. Caller 9's mouth went dry, his next question caught momentarily in his throat. He was about to ask a naughty question. A terrible moment flashed through his mind as he imagined his secret being revealed. For a millisecond he could imagine the shame, the disgrace, the congressional ethics panel hearings. Shame became pleasure. He thought the phone service was worth every penny.

'Is your big ass full, Black Mistress Tina?' Girl 39 wiped some guacamole from her shirt sleeve – shit she had just had the blouse cleaned.

'Yeah, it's full you dumb slave fuck.'

Caller 9 leaned forward on his chair. He stared at the Washington Monument as his hand fell to his lap. 'I'd like you to toilet train me Black Mistress Tina.'

Girl 39 bunched up the wrapping papers from her dinner and tossed them into the garbage. She wiped a few crumbs from the desk top into the trash can.

'We'll see what I'm in the mood for, sweetheart. Do you have any toys?'

Caller 9 had toys and couldn't wait to tell Black Mistress Tina about each and every one of them.

Girl 6 was not on the phone. She was waiting for a request from Caller 1 – Bob from Tucson. Bob was a regular, every other night at the same time. Girl 6 sat at her station sipping a can of Diet Pepsi and watching the clock on her computer monitor tick down. Girl 19 finished her session with Martin and Christine and said her goodbyes. She made a few notes in her caller log and leaned over the partition that separated their cubicles.

'They say the same old shit every week. You ever married?'

'Two years to a real loser.' Girl 6 didn't like to talk about it.

Girl 19 wanted to know more. 'No kids?'

Girl 6 was prepping herself for Bob from Tucson. It was a quarter till the hour – why hadn't he called? Did he have a problem? Had something happened? Did Bob from Tucson have a problem with her? That was the worst scenario. Had he grown bored with her? Had she said something wrong? Had Bob from Tucson found somebody new?

Girl 6 barely heard Girl 19's question. She answered on auto pilot. 'Nope. No kids.'

Girl 19 must have been really bored by Martin and Christine. She wouldn't shut up. 'Was the love good?'

'Not bad.' That had been the one halfway decent memory from the marriage.

Girl 19 was unstoppable. 'Miss him?'

'Nope.'

'Ever see him?'

'Last week on *America's Most Wanted*.'

Both women had to laugh. Girl 6 got her confidence back. She pulled Bob's card from her caller box. There was nothing to worry about. He'd call.

Girl 6's phone flashed. She plugged herself in and picked up the receiver. She didn't wait to hear his voice. 'Bob.'

'Lovely.' It was Bob. He was happy to hear Girl 6's voice.

'I missed you.' Girl 6 wasn't quite speaking from her heart – but she wasn't quite acting either.

Somewhere between Tucson and Phoenix, on Interstate 10, Caller 1 drove with one hand and held his car phone in the other. The desert was barren with winter and there wasn't much for him to look at.

'I missed you too. You won't believe where I'm calling from.'

Girl 6 could guess. She had become an expert in figuring out where people called from. Sometimes they called from the strangest places. A car phone was no big deal.

'Ya calling from your car?'

Caller 1 didn't know how she knew – he had spent a lot of money on buying the best new car phone that he could find. Girl 6 was smart and he liked that.

'Can I talk about my mom?'

Girl 6 ran a finger down Caller 1's index card. She noted that

70

Caller 1's mother had been pretty sick. 'She's still in the hospital, right?'

Caller 1 felt good when Girl 6 remembered. Girl 6 cared about him. She wasn't just another phone-sex operator. Sure, she could do a good job getting him off, but Caller 1 knew in his heart that their relationship wasn't just about the money. He could talk to her, share his thoughts with her. Caller 1 had a difficult time doing this with a lot of women. In fact Caller 1 felt the relationship he had with Girl 6 was more fulfilling than any relationship he had ever had with a flesh and blood woman. She remembered his problems, remembered what he liked, even though she must talk with a lot of guys. Girl 6 had proved to Bob from Tucson that she cared.

'Yeah – still in the hospital. She's not too good. It's not like she and I were ever close. She never had a kind word for me. I dunno why I'm even making the effort.'

Girl 6 said something that made Caller 1's week: 'Relationships change. Look at you and me. When we started it was just for sex.'

Caller 1 didn't realize it, but suddenly he was speeding way above the limit.

'And now we're talking about my mother.'

Girl 6 knew what he wanted to hear next. 'The sex is still hot, baby.'

Caller 1 couldn't keep his mind on his driving. He was in love and had to do something about it.

'Yeah, it is. I'm gonna pull over, okay?' Caller 1 hit the brakes and pulled on to the side of the road.

# CHAPTER TWELVE

Girl 6 was in the middle of a long shift. She unplugged herself from the system and was ready to take fifteen minutes off, get some fresh air and buy some stuff downstairs at the Indian's convenience store. On her way out she stopped in the lounge, opened the worn refrigerator and took out the second half of the meatball sub she had bought for lunch. She could heat it up in the microwave later and have it for dinner. Girl 6 always liked to have at least one hot meal a day. She took her coffee mug, dumped the contents, rinsed it out and hung it to dry next to the others. It was time to switch to Coke for the rest of the shift. A few weeks back Lil had provided each woman with her own mug personalized with the woman's number painted in florid, pink nail polish. As Girl 6 washed out the sink, the timer on the coffee machine clicked on – another automatically brewed pot was in the works. Girl 6 went to a row of grey mini-lockers, spun a multicolored combination lock and removed her jacket. She looked at the lockers for a moment, thought about laughing, but was too tired to make the effort. Each unit had a tag with a childishly drawn number on the colored paper. Each looked different and was tied through the locker's little air vents with a string. Lil had wanted each woman to make their own sign. She felt it was good for the company spirit to have each woman express something of her own individual personality.

As Girl 6 neatened her personal items, Lil entered the room and began to tape up freshly made signs. When the women on the next shift arrived they'd be surprised and pleased by the new awards. Girl 6 shut her locker and took a look.

TOP GIRLS THIS PAY PERIOD Most Calls: Girl 5. Most Minutes: Girl 23. Most Requests: Girl 42. Most Improved Calls:

Girl 19. Most Improved Minutes: Girl 42. Most Improved Requests: Girl 39. $50 Bonus to all! Congratulations!!!

Lil gauged Girl 6's reaction. The signs were good for the girls' morale. They gave the girls goals, motivation. Lil knew that Girl 6 was doing a good job – better than a good job. She also knew that Girl 6 could be pushed to do even more. Girl 6 was hungry for something and Lil knew how to turn that desire into cash.

'You wanna make money, you'd take it.' Lil had been on Girl 6's ass to pick up another shift. There was no one in Girl 6's cubicle for the next shift and Lil thought it was time to push her. Sure, Lil understood that Girl 6 was tired, but so what?

Girl 6 was worn down and didn't have a lot of fight left in her. She hadn't had a day off in a long time and couldn't face the thought of staying through another shift. She wanted to go home at the end of this one. She deserved a decent break.

'I'm beat as it is.'

Lil stepped up the cheerful pressure. 'It's money. Hold this for me, huh?' Girl 6 held the new poster against the wall while Lil taped it into place. Lil wasn't feeling subtle. She had shoved the facts and figures right in Girl 6's face.

Girl 6 tried to talk around the subject. 'You like Didi? My red-head? She's new.'

Lil wasn't the type to be bullshitted. 'She's fine. I need you to fill this shift. It's a good shift and it could put you in line for a bonus.' Lil paused and pressed Girl 6's buttons – it was easy to do. 'You still planning on LA?'

Girl 6 was. Lil played her hand.

'You wanna get out? The only way out is in, honey.'

Girl 6 was a determined woman though, and knew what Lil was trying to do. She wasn't going to give in too easily.

'Lemme think about it, okay?' Lil shrugged. She could wait. She was a determined woman too.

Girl 6 went back into the lounge. Girl 4 and Girl 39 were talking. The silent television played some stupid romantic TV

73

melodrama. Girl 4 watched it, not caring about the dialogue. No television writer in Hollywood could compete with the trashy dialogue that constantly ran through Girl 4's head nowadays. She got a kick out of putting her own words in the actors' mouths. Girl 39 ate a mocha-chip ice-cream cone with sprinkles. Her throat hurt from talking too much and all the cigarette smoke in the operators' room. Lil herself had gone out to get Girl 39 something that would make her feel better. Girl 39 appreciated Lil's pampering. The cold felt great. Girl 39 was beginning to feel like she could sex for a few more hours.

Girl 39 tested out her recovering vocal chords. 'Young guys are the worst. They come too fast – Hi there, my name's – BANG and then they hang up.'

Girl 4 looked up, agreeing and adding with a laugh, 'They sure call a lot, though.'

Girl 39 laughed. 'It's a trade off. Wanna watch TV?'

Girl 4 had to be back on the phones in ten minutes. Girl 39 tossed her some earphones and changed the channels, finding an old black and white movie. 'So watch for ten.'

Girl 4 preferred the television without sound but didn't want to make Girl 39 think she didn't appreciate her concern. Girl 4 plugged herself in and the two of them sat back and watched Fredric March woo Greta Garbo. The women here didn't need a matinée idol to take care of them. They took care of each other.

Girl 6 stepped into the lounge. 'It's my turn out. Anything? Cigarettes?' But Girls 4 and 39 were mesmerized by the celluloid passion and never even noticed her.

Girl 6 went downstairs to the Pearl of Bombay Magazine Emporium. It was a small, cluttered shop with racks of magazines, newspapers, videos, junk food, cigarettes, condoms, over-the-counter medications, postcards and strange items that the owner must have gotten really cheap because Girl 6 couldn't figure out why he thought anybody would buy them – cheap metal 'sculptures' of people, 'trophies' from the 1980 Moscow Olympics – a bizarre variety of useless merchandise. Girl 6 thought it was amazing what some people would spend their money on.

The shopkeeper was an immigrant from India and had two golden teeth. Wearing a flimsy shirt made of a material that rustled like paper, the shopkeeper was exceedingly proud of his chest hair. He made sure he displayed it by leaving the top three buttons on his cheap shirt unbuttoned. Girl 6 usually only came into the shop late at night, and once she had actually caught him combing his chest hair. Girl 6 had the feeling that he wanted her to catch him in the act. He hadn't been embarrassed at all and she let the moment pass.

Girl 6 asked the shopkeeper for a variety of cigarettes. Each woman upstairs had her own preference, although when everyone lit up, the smoke seemed to mix together into a single mongrel flavor. Somehow cigarette brands were part of the women's identities. If they didn't have names, they had name brands, and that seemed to help. Girl 6 ignored all the new yuppie brands and stuck with her old reliable Marlboros. Girl 6 always laughed whenever Girl 19 lifted her pinky finger as she dragged on an Elegance cigarette. They were all made by the same manufacturers. The only real difference was the packaging, or so Girl 6 had heard. She didn't care to try them all herself. As she figured it, the only difference came from the suggestive imagery of the ad campaigns. She spun bullshit for a living and knew it when she heard it. Marlboros were just fine with her.

As the shopkeeper assembled the list of cigarettes, Girl 6's eyes wandered to an area above the counter. A sign was nailed to the wall that had a police drawing of the shoplifter displayed. Korean letters shouted something. Although Girl 6 had recently added a Thai sex-tour masseuse named Lotus Blossom to her repertoire – she still couldn't read Korean. Girl 6 noted the picture of the shoplifter, however, and caught the general drift. When she looked closer, Girl 6 saw a handprinted English translation – 'Thief, Beware!' Girl 6 noted that the shoplifter was expanding his territory. The shopkeeper placed the last of the cigarettes on the counter. Girl 6 asked for plenty of matches.

Girl 6 let her eyes wander to the glossy magazines. *Cosmopolitan*, *Mirabelle*, *GQ*, *Elle*. Cindy Crawford looked out from the gilded confines of her cover in all her absolute perfection. Girl 6 felt a momentary pang. She knew she was pretty but she also knew that any of her past lovers would have dropped her in a second for a night with the supermodel. Girl 6 consoled herself with the knowledge that, without the makeup, lights and airbrushing, Cindy Crawford was probably no more beautiful than she was. Cindy Crawford had her makeup artist, Girl 6 had her voice. The difference between reality and flawlessness was illusion.

Girl 6 liked the idea that the women on the magazine covers were doing something pretty similar to her own job. All of Girl 6's sex talk was there on the magazines' front covers. When you came right down to it, Girl 6 wasn't all that different from Cindy, Elle or Linda after all. She just used a different method of performance. She repeated the thought in her head over and over like a mantra that could make something true by repetition. At some core level, however, Girl 6 didn't really buy it. Girl 6 knew – illusions and rationalizations aside – that Cindy, Elle and Linda were different. They lived rarified lives. They lived in a world she could only dream of. If Girl 6 spun fantasies that helped lonely men feel there was someone out there who cared for them, then these hip goddesses, these leather-skirted, lip-glossed Aphrodites proved to Girl 6 that her fantasies weren't fiction at all. If she got enough guys to pay her to give life to their desires, Girl 6 would eventually get to step across the threshold of her gray, dispirited world and into the vivid, never-ending party of Cindy, Elle and Linda's.

'You're a snow bunny?' Girl 6 was ripped out of her own pastel-colored reverie and found herself back in the gold-toothed Indian's magazine emporium. She wasn't the only one in the store with an ambitious sense of self. The shopkeeper asked her again, 'You like skiing? You're a snow bunny?'

Girl 6 was a little dazed by the culture shock between where she had been and where she was now. She didn't like skiing.

The shopkeeper was persistent. 'You like to fish?'

Girl 6 had been fishing as a little girl with her father. 'It's okay.' Girl 6 wasn't in the mood to talk about fishing. She was, however, vaguely interested in the 'Thief, Beware' sign.

'Who's he?'

She could see the anger flare in the shopkeeper's face. 'Bad news. Black bastard. No offense.'

The shopkeeper swerved back to his original line of questioning. 'I'll take you fishing. I have a friend with a cabin on a lake. You and I and a rowboat for two.'

Girl 6 might have laughed, but right now she just wanted to get out of the store. 'How much?'

For the moment, the shopkeeper wasn't interested in his receipts. 'You work upstairs?'

Girl 6 knew what he was about. She wanted no part of it. He had a pretty fucked-up idea of who she was. 'How much?'

The shopkeeper was lost in his own conversation. 'What's your number? Maybe we could talk sometime, I call you Hot Mama.' The shopkeeper reached across the counter and grabbed Girl 6's arm. 'Come on, Hot Mama, gimme some sex. I close up for ten minutes. We go in back, on cot.'

Girl 6 pushed his arm away and held up some cash for the shopkeeper to see. Maybe that would return his attention to where it belonged. It didn't work.

'I'm a rich man. You won't have to work. You like to go fishing?'

Maybe fishing was part of the mating ritual in India, but Girl 6 just wanted out.

'Don't forget the matches.'

The shopkeeper took his best shot. 'Lucky girl, beautiful lucky girl. You could be my beautiful bride, my wife. I'm talking matrimony!'

Girl 6 had heard enough. 'Oh, fuck off!'

The shopkeeper understood. His romantic ambitions were doused. She was just a whore. He went back to a subject that whores understood.

'Forty-three dollars, forty-eight cents.'

Girl 6 glared at him as she paid. She knew what he thought about her. What an ignorant asshole. He was too fucking stupid to know the difference between what she said and what she actually did. The shopkeeper was afraid to lose her business, but he also still wanted to fuck her on a moldy cot stuck between cartons of Cheez-its and caffeine-free colas.

'I apologize, you got me worked up. You give me number, I call. We have phone sex first.'

Girl 6 looked at him like he was crazy. Was he just being a sarcastic prick or did he actually think that would work with her? Girl 6 didn't know and didn't really care. Fuck him. She walked out and leaned against the walls of the magazine emporium.

This had turned out to be some break. Girl 6 was exhausted. She caught her breath and then went back to work, having made a decision.

Girl 6 walked up the two flights of stairs and directly into Lil's office. Lil sat behind her desk wearing bifocals, doing paperwork. She knew exactly what Girl 6 was about to tell her. Girl 6 put a hand on Lil's shoulder. 'I'll take it. The extra shift.'

Lil was happy to hear it. Girl 6 quoted something Lil said earlier, as though to convince herself of having made the right choice: 'The only way out is in.'

Lil swiveled in her chair and stroked Girl 6's cheek maternally. 'Good girl.'

# CHAPTER THIRTEEN

While most of the women were finishing their overnight shift, Girl 6 was just beginning her extra eight hours. It was a few minutes before seven in the morning and most of her co-workers were cleaning up their stations and getting ready to leave. Girl 4 whispered good night. Girl 39 smiled sympathetically as she left the room. Girl 6 would have loved to go home. She would have loved not to talk to anyone. Girl 6 knew, however, that her voice couldn't reflect her fatigue. She had to be on. She had to make the guys think she gave a shit. She had to make them come and she had to make them come back for more. Girl 6 had a new caller on the phone. He sounded like he had some potential. By now Girl 6 could tell from a caller's voice whether or not he had money. She could tell whether or not the guy was a serious caller or if it was just a one-time thing – some curious guy who happened to be flipping through the back pages of the kind of paper that advertised 900 numbers.

Girl 6 began with a neutral sports question. She was working by the book and sports were Lil's first subject suggestion. 'How-about them Knicks, huh?' Caller 12 was thrilled to talk to a girl who loved sports. Caller 12 loved sports. He knew he could talk with Lovely Brown – the Girl Next Door.

Caller 12 sat behind his gorgeous desk and looked out at the view from his Ninety-First Street penthouse. Dawn came late at this time of year and the cloudy morning kept it darker than it really should have been. A dulled hangover sunrise was just beginning to compete with the night lights of Manhattan.

Caller 12 rolled a small Nerf basketball across the desk top. 'I was at the Garden last night. The law firm owns one of those skyboxes. I'm a partner. You ought to join me sometime, Lovely.'

Girl 6 forced herself to be fun. 'That would be a flagrant foul.'

Caller 12 appreciated a girl who could be funny. A lot of women he talked to on the 900 lines didn't have much of a sense of humor.

Caller 12 responded playfully in a sing songy voice, 'We could have fu-unnnn.'

Girl 6 was working hard to make sure Caller 12 did have some fun. 'I caught the highlights on MSG. They were hot!'

Caller 12 wished Girl 6 had been at the game and then shot his Nerf basketball across the room and through a plastic hoop sticking to the wall. 'Starks drained that three pointer. What a beauty. Nothing but net.'

Girl 6 had seen part of the game in the lounge. 'And at the buzzer.'

Caller 12 had the right girl on the phone. He shot again and scored. 'Feels like '69–'70 all over again.'

Girl 6 didn't know what had actually happened in '69–'70. She remembered that the Miracle Mets had taken the World Series. Girl 6 figured the Knicks must have had that kind of season too.

'I was thinking the same thing. Think they'll go all the way?' Good. She was proud of herself. That had been a safely generic response. She never liked having to pretend she knew something about a subject that she was actually pretty clueless about. It was too easy to get caught in the lie and that was often a turn off to the caller. Trust was a big deal to the callers.

Caller 12's mind moved off the basketball court. 'All the way? Think we will? I got a beautiful hard rod for you, Lovely. And you need it bad, dontcha, bitch?'

Girl 6 was pleased. She was on safer ground now. She had led Caller 12 where she wanted him to go.

Girl 42 headed for the door, turned around and handed Girl 6 an envelope while she whispered good night. Girl 6 gave Girl 42 a quick, envious wave and returned her attention to Caller 12.

'Yes, I do. Yes, I do. You'd be watching the game and I'd be sucking you off right in the skybox. I'm a lottery pick.'

Caller 12 imagined himself at the Garden. Woody and the other stars might sit on the floor, but the hardwood was a pretty indiscreet place if you had lovers like Lovely Brown.

'Put me in your mouth, girl. And let me milk them big b-ball tits. Cuz I got game. I'd slam dunk on you 24–7.' In his mind the crowds were cheering, Lovely Brown was taking him towards the basket. 'I'd do a crossover dribble, Lovely, then take it into the paint, go strong into the hole. PRIMETIME.'

Caller 12 sighed fiercely and came – nothing but net.

Things had gotten busy after Caller 12, and Girl 6 had forgotten to look at Girl 42's envelope. It wasn't until early afternoon that Girl 6 even remembered that she had it. Girl 6 was talking to Caller 13 about the pilgrims. She had pulled out Caller 13's card to add this new area of interest for future reference when the file box tipped over. Girl 42's envelope sat there unopened as Girl 6 sexed Caller 13. Apparently, Caller 13 was a real blue blood.

'My mother's family came over on the Mayflower.'

'That's really hot.' Girl 6 ripped open the envelope. She looked inside and pulled out a neatly folded article on Angela King – the little girl who had fallen down the elevator shaft.

She listened to Caller 13's history lesson.

'They were actually a very sexually active bunch of people. The religion thing was just a cover.'

'That's really hot. That's really hot.' Girl 6 was excruciatingly tired. She was having a tough time being creative. She looked at a photograph taken of Angela sitting on Santa's lap at a community center.

Caller 13 didn't seem to notice her lack of originality. He was feeling creative enough for the two of them.

'You bet. So let's say I'm, like, Miles Standish and you're Pocahontas. And you want me really bad.'

Caller 13 began to unravel his pilgrim fantasy. He seemed to be happy with Girl 6's limited contribution to the conversation. Girl 6 was relieved that all Caller 13 seemed to want was an audience while he and the Indian maiden re-wrote the

Thanksgiving legend. Girl 6 let her mind wander and moaned occasionally when it seemed appropriate. She read Girl 42's newspaper clipping. Apparently little Angela wasn't doing well at all. She hadn't regained consciousness and wasn't expected to any time soon. Her brain function was limited and she was on life support. Her mother, father, and family members sat vigil at her bedside. Mayor Giulani, Cardinal O'Connor, Congressman Rangel, Patrick Ewing, Lawrence Taylor, Reverend Sharpton, Salt 'n Peppa and various other luminaries had visited her. Nita Hicks, the first television reporter, had been joined by journalists from all of the city's papers and stations. But Girl 6 didn't need all of them to tell her what an awful tragedy it was. She already knew. Girl 6 stared at Angela's picture and was unexpectedly, profoundly, grief-stricken. She couldn't say exactly why she felt so terrible – innocent children died in her community with an appalling regularity. There was something about this particular little girl. Girl 6 felt as if something in herself had been lost. She remembered her dream of falling through the elevator shaft and felt a premonition of the void.

# CHAPTER FOURTEEN

The shift hadn't ended yet. It was early afternoon and Girl 6 was still working. Girl 39 sat in the cubicle next to Girl 6 as they performed a two-girl call with Caller 14. Girl 6 spoke fearfully.

'What if someone catches us?'

Girl 39 acted as the more confident, more mature one of the pair. 'No one's gonna catch us.'

'I'm nervous. Oh, I'm nervous, Cindy,' Girl 6 said with a high-school-girl's panic as she stared straight ahead, concentrating.

Girl 39 looked at an Avon catalogue and found a new lipstick that looked like a good shade for her. 'Melissa, we're in the girl's bathroom and everyone else is in class. I'm gonna stick my hand up your skirt.'

'Oooooh . . .' Girl 6 moaned happily.

Caller 14 offered a personal status report: 'That's good! I'm so big it's deformed.'

As the women took Caller 14 along on his fantasy trip, Salesgirl 2 approached their cubicles. She flashed a hand-drawn sign that read, 'WE'RE TAPING!' This was good news: a recognition of a job well done. Girl 39 smiled. Girl 6 offered an enthusiastic thumbs up.

Girl 39 felt inspired. 'Unbutton your blouse, Melissa. I've been thinking about your tits all day. All through math class and history class. Show 'em to me.'

Caller 14 was really getting into it and shouted in a tiny voice, 'Yeah, show 'em to me!!'

Girl 39 put down her Avon catalogue, leaned over the partition, crossed her eyes, pushed up her nose with her free hand, and blew out her cheeks.

'Oh, Missy, your tits are so yummy I wanna rub my wet hot pink pussy all over your nipples.' Girl 39 had a tough time holding back her laughter. If Caller 14 hadn't been so involved doing whatever exactly it was that he was doing, he surely would have heard the change in her voice.

Girl 6 didn't even acknowledge Girl 39's funny face. She'd seen it but it hadn't really registered in her mind. She was totally focused on her work – lost within Missy.

Girl 39 tapped Girl 6 on the shoulder and tried to break her concentration. It worked. Girl 6 jumped in her seat and looked up – as though she were surprised to find herself in the office. Girl 39 shrugged and went back to her Avon catalogue. Her sister had told her something about a new eye-liner. That's how wildly bored she was: she was actually paying attention to a makeup suggestion from her sister. Girl 39 didn't really give a shit about makeup. Her sister lived with her husband and five children in Jersey and thought makeup, clothes, hair were all exceptionally important. Girl 39's sister had started sending her various catalogues and magazines – *Avon*, *Victoria's Secret*, *Martha Stewart* – hoping to get Girl 39 married and settled down. It wasn't working.

Distracted, Girl 6 took out her caller minutes sheet and began to tally up what she had earned so far. She tapped her fingers on the desk as she counted. A moment later she stopped, unable to count correctly. She was losing herself again. Unconsciously she put her pen to another task. Girl 6 began to write something on her minutes sheet and responded to Girl 39's last dialogue. 'Cindy, you're such a hot slut. Get on top of me.'

Girl 39 noticed that her hands were looking rough. She'd have to buy some moisturizing lotion on the way home.

'Missy, your tits are so big. I'm gonna come.'

From somewhere across America, Caller 14 altered his voice – he sounded entirely different.

'What do you two girls think you're doing?!'

Girl 6 had been through this fantasy before. 'Cindy, it's Mr Blue, the custodian!'

Caller 14 returned to his normal speaking voice and gave stage directions. 'And this is where I take out my huge cock.' Caller 14 switched back to Mr Blue's voice and spoke enticingly to the two girls he had just caught. 'See my big cock?'

Girl 39 passed a scrap of paper over the cubicle divider. It read, 'Mr Blue?!' Girl 6 shrugged her shoulders. She was well acquainted with Mr Blue.

'Suck me off, the both of you, or I'm telling the principal,' Mr Blue yelled at them angrily. 'Suck me off! Suck me off!'.

Girl 6 put down her pen and began to suck Mr Blue off. The piece of paper was covered with a repetitive coupling of names – MISS CINDY MR BLUE MISS CINDY MR BLUE MISS CINDY MR BLUE MISS CINDY MR BLUE MISS CINDY MR BLUE MISS CINDY MR BLUE MISS CINDY MR BLUE.

It was much later. Girl 6 was in her fourteenth hour on the job. She and Girl 39 sat in the lounge completely beat. All the other women had gone home. There was no one calling. Girl 39 smoked a butt and handed Girl 6 a tape.

'Borrow it for one week for ten dollars. Study it good and it'll raise your requests 50 per cent in two weeks, guaranteed.'

Girl 6 looked at the cassette with a tired interest.

'I could be like Brigitte Bardot.'

'Yep. Money back guarantee. How close are you?'

Girl 6 yawned. 'I thought I'd split in a few months but it doesn't look that way. I'm beat but it's not so bad. Bob from Tucson wants to meet me in person. I gave him my phone number.'

Girl 39 breathed the cigarette smoke deeply into her lungs. She still wasn't one for giving advice, but she thought that Girl 6 was slipping further into a trap. She had to say something, even if Girl 6 hadn't listened to her the last time. The smoke made her feel better about playing big sister. It was as though the act helped Girl 39 maintain her self-image of being cool, knowing, sophisticated – it protected her from showing that she worried about how all this stuff could affect people.

'Don't get hooked on this talking stuff. It's just talk.'

A few months back Girl 6 would have automatically agreed. She couldn't agree anymore.

'He's got a great voice.' Girl 6 looked forward to Bob from Tuscon's calls. In a crowd of grunting men, Bob stood apart. Bob didn't just want to get off. Bob needed her. She knew stuff about him and he knew stuff about her. She knew what he liked. He was always appreciative, always attentive to her mood or degree of exhaustion. Girl 6 was grateful when Bob told her not to say anything one time when she was totally beat. He stayed on the line, making her money, and told her about his life. She knew more about Bob than she did about her ex-husband. Bob from Tucson wasn't just another loser. Girl 39 saw the look in Girl 6's eyes and figured it wouldn't do.

'I ever tell you about the girl who got hooked?'

Before Girl 39 could tell her story the computer monitor insert on the TV began flashing Girl 6's number. She was relieved. She didn't want a lecture. She could handle whatever came her way. Girl 6 got to her feet, happy to be headed back to the phones.

'I'm up. Training bra fantasy. Lucky me.'

# CHAPTER FIFTEEN

Girl 6 had the day off and was spending it with her neighbor Jimmy. She had been making some good money and took Jimmy out for lunch at a Cuban diner on 122nd Street. The upbeat music playing in the background suited her mood. She was thrilled not to be working the phones. It had been a long time since she had a free day. Girl 6 was sick of sandwiches and had the barbecued pork special, plantains, and flan for dessert. The flan was especially good. Its sweetness coated her raw, over-worked throat.

They walked uptown after their meal and checked out the window displays. Girl 6 led a reluctant Jimmy into her favorite wig shop. He was amazed to find rack after rack of differently styled wigs. He had no idea there were so many variations to choose from. Jimmy began to wonder about the women he knew and the women he had known. How many had been wearing costumes, altering themselves in a small way, wearing slight disguises, playing roles?

Girl 6 and Jimmy looked over the selection – fifties wigs, sixties wigs – styles that were all before their time. Both recognized the seventies section with its huge afros and faded pictures of 'Black and proud' seventies sisters. Girl 6 passed the punk section with its neon blue, green and pink combinations and thought of buying one as a joke for Girl 39.

Jimmy showed Girl 6 a 'Real Hair' section. He looked at the wigs carefully and touched them. He made a face and jumped back. Jimmy didn't like the idea of touching some real person's hair. Who had it belonged to? How had the wigmaker gotten it? He pulled Girl 6 to another aisle.

Girl 6 made Jimmy stop at the historical section. They looked at re-creations from the seventeenth, eighteenth and nineteenth

87

centuries before going back to the afros. Girl 6 put on a huge afro and showed Jimmy. He thought it was great.

'Style it.' Girl 6 did as he asked.

Jimmy was having a great time. 'It's you. It's really you.'

Girl 6 laughed but it was forced. Her mind was somewhere else – with someone other than Jimmy.

'He's missed two nights now. What's his fucking problem?'

The question pissed Jimmy off but he didn't let himself show it. 'Maybe his mom died.'

Jimmy tried to stop the conversation before it began. He thought his response might shut Girl 6 up. It didn't. Girl 6 turned to him. She fidgeted nervously.

'If she croaked he woulda called. He helped her pick out her casket, and who helped him help her? Lovely Brown did.'

Jimmy and Girl 6 walked down Broadway. Neither was happy with the other. Jimmy had looked forward to spending the day with Girl 6 and it didn't please him that he had to share her company with someone else. Someone she had never actually met. Someone who she seemed to be growing pretty close to. Jimmy gave Girl 6 some good-natured shit. He was mad but he could see the humor in the situation. Jimmy was in control of himself. When Jimmy suggested that the reason Bob might not have called was because he might have gotten married, Girl 6 was furious.

'What do you mean, maybe he got married?'

Jimmy couldn't believe Girl 6 could get jealous over some loser who paid her to talk to him.

'Just an idea.' He had grown tired of the conversation.

Girl 6 was really pissed off at Jimmy and wasn't going to let it pass. 'You're always bringing me down. I work like a dog and I wanna talk about it and you bring me down.'

Jimmy couldn't believe that this fucking Bob guy was competition. What the fuck was wrong with Girl 6? He said he didn't want to talk about it, but he did.

'It's just making you kooky, that's all. Yer his main girl,

okay? Try talking about something else sometimes, that's all.'

Girl 6 had to talk about it. She was upset and she had to try and talk it through.

'There's nothing else to talk about. Nothing else goes on.'

'Bullshit.' Jimmy didn't believe her and couldn't understand how she could be talking such shit.

Girl 6 tried to convince him. 'No lie.'

Jimmy was fucking fed up. Girl 6 wasn't the girl she used to be, she wasn't the girl he used to know. 'Then try just quiet for five minutes.'

Girl 6 took enough instructions from guys when she was at work. She didn't care to take orders when she was on her own time. 'Let's try talking about how much money you owe me.'

'Wait a minute. I don't owe you that much.' Jimmy knew she was trying to get him mad but it still worked. Girl 6 was blind to what was in front of her. Here he was, a decent enough guy, and she was more interested in some asshole from Tucson who liked to jack off to her voice. Things were fucked. 'Besides, I care about you. On the up and up.' He meant it.

'Yeah, like a sow loves her slops, man.'

They walked home silently. Arriving at the New Amsterdam Royal they found the shoplifter waiting by the front door. He held a package in his hands. Jimmy went upstairs without saying another word to Girl 6. That was fine with her. She looked at the shoplifter sadly. He looked at her. Girl 6 wondered what he was up to. What was with the package? She was sure he had stolen it for her. What a thoughtful prince of a guy.

The shoplifter spoke earnestly. 'Before you say anything I got a little something I want to give you. No, I didn't steal it. It's kind of funny because this old man gave this to me.'

Girl 6 listened but didn't believe him. Sure, some old man had just walked up to him on the street and gave him a package. The shoplifter must have thought she was pretty stupid, pretty naïve. Maybe she had been at one time. She wasn't anymore.

The shoplifter had been staring into her eyes meaningfully. He broke eye contact and continued his story. 'He was kinda weird. He used to dream that once he became a famous actor he would get to marry a beautiful movie star. He used to say that if you want something really bad, you just get a picture of it and hang it up on your wall and look at it every day.'

Girl 6 couldn't figure if the shoplifter was bullshitting her or not. Maybe he didn't even know that he was spinning bullshit. He was hitting too close to home with his wanna-be actor who figured everything would turn out when he finally made it as a star. He was too on target when he talked about the pictures on the wall that you were supposed to stare at every day. Or maybe he just had a memory that was for shit.

Girl 6 was about to tell him off when he gave her a mint-condition copy of a 1941 *Look* magazine. The cover picture was of Dorothy Dandridge. She had never looked better. She was a black Rita Hayworth, a Marilyn Monroe. Men would go to war and die fighting for that image. Dandridge made Cindy, Elle and Linda look like pasty schoolgirls. Dandridge had it. Girl 6 wanted it. All she had to do was keep working. In the meantime, the shoplifter had given her a terrific gift. Maybe one of the best she'd ever received. The shoplifter understood her – at least that part of her. She was grateful, thrilled and moved by his attention.

'Since you're acting, maybe this will help you out,' the shoplifter explained. 'I never had anybody give me anything before, so I've been taking stuff all my life. Hope you like it.'

'I love it.'

The shoplifter showed his hand. 'Can I come up?'

Girl 6 shouldn't have been surprised. She should have picked up on the shoplifter's line of shit when he told her nobody had ever given him anything. Girl 6 knew that wasn't the case. Girl 6 knew that the shoplifter had lifted the *Look* magazine hoping to fuck her. She wasn't interested.

'I'm busy right now.'

90

'I was just wondering.' The shoplifter acted as though he hadn't planned the whole scenario, as though the idea of sleeping with her had just struck him out of the blue.

Girl 6 was coldly polite knowing he had constructed the whole sequence ahead of time in his mind. 'Thank you for the magazine.'

She went inside the building leaving the shoplifter out in the cold.

# CHAPTER SIXTEEN

Girl 6 and Girl 42 helped themselves to coffee in the lounge. Girl 4 was watching television, listening to a sitcom over earphones. Girl 39 and Girl 29 walked in talking.

'He was an axe murderer. He was calling me from prison.'

'And you talked to him?' Girl 29 was shocked. That was the kind of call they were allowed to pass on.

'Hottest call I ever had. Gimme a bite.' Girl 6 offered her a bite of an ice-cream cone that Girl 42 had just bought for her. Girl 39 wanted her tape back from Girl 6.

'I need another week.'

Girl 39 didn't want the extra ten bucks. She wanted her tape back before she got rusty.

'No interest, *amiga*.'

Girl 42 thought the whole tape business was a waste of time. 'Guys don't fall for that French shit.'

Girl 6 thought they did. 'You'd be surprised.'

It wasn't a big deal either way. Girl 39 continued telling Girl 29 about her convict caller.

'He was into escape fantasies. I'd be the warden's wife. Come into the jail to find a real man 'cause the warden couldn't get it up, right? And he would have me through the bars of his cell. I'd pull down the front of my low-cut red dress, stick my huge tits through the bars, then hold on and he'd do me.'

Girl 6 listened to some of Girl 39's story. It sounded to her like Girl 39 was making the same mistake that she tried to warn Girl 6 about. It was some story. Girl 39 smiled at Girl 6, acknowledging her double standard.

'I would come with this guy we had such a hot talk.'

Girl 29 was impressed. She'd have liked the convict to call her too. 'What happened to him?'

Girl 39 put on her serious face. 'Lethal injection. They kill you quick in the state of Texas.'

Girl 6 could see the joke in Girl 39's eyes. Girl 29 didn't realize it was a joke, though. She felt a little depressed – the convict would never be calling her. All she could say was, 'Oh.'

Girl 39 played her along. 'Hot rod, lemme tell ya.' She was on a roll. This would be a good night for Girl 39.

Girl 42 grabbed her coat. 'It's my turn to go out. You guys want?'

'No, thanks.' Girl 42 couldn't get what Girl 29 wanted at the Indian magazine store.

'Smokes. Three packs.' Girl 39 was pulling a double and needed something to help her get through it. Girl 42 didn't need to ask the brand. She knew. Girl 42 took the money and walked out the door. Girl 39 couldn't stop talking. 'I got this guy who likes smoke blown in his face.'

Girl 6 didn't hear anything more. She had plugged in the television earphones and was watching a news report. Nita Hicks sat in the waiting room at Mount Sinai hospital. Angela King's mother was stunned with grief – her eyes thick with red veins from endless crying. Angela's aunt, a spluttering, hefty volcano of barely restrained rage, sat next to her. Angela's mother and aunt held hands. Some time in the future, when the crisis was over, Angela's mother was going to wonder why her fingers were so bruised. Nita Hicks's face showed an appropriate combination of sympathetic sadness and the required strength of a veteran television journalist. Her producer had coached after the first few reports that her obvious anguish was bordering on the unprofessional. Nita Hicks's credibility as a journalist compelled her to control her emotions in front of the camera. Angela's accident, something that had originally seemed nothing more than a career opportunity, had affected Hicks in a way she hadn't thought possible. She was also getting national air time.

'We're waiting, still hoping, still praying. There iduhn't much we can do but that.' Hicks asked a question but didn't bother with a cut away. The camera stayed on the grieving women – an unprecedented decision by the producer.

'Your daughter was making what looked like a miraculous recovery. And we all hoped she'd be released very soon.'

Angela's mother couldn't respond. It was all too horribly true. Angela had regained consciousness and had called for her mother and father. Then she had slipped away again – lost in an ambiguous place between life and nothingness. Angela's mother's whole body heaved as the tears erupted convulsively from her. Angela's aunt squeezed her sister tight and answered for her.

'It don't look that way now. Don't look like Angie's ever gonna come home now, does it?'

Angela's mother had to speak. She couldn't be silent when her baby was suffering. She had to let the people know who was looking out for her child. It was as if by stating the fact, it would suddenly be so. 'We sent it up to Jesus – it's in the Lord's hands.'

The producer couldn't resist a cut away. A second camera showed Nita Hicks nodding. Someone watching would know that in her mind Hicks was saying, 'Amen.' Nita Hicks might have been a nineties woman – a hardened newsperson, successful in her career and glamorous – but the producer also knew that it was crucial for her to be known as the kid next door who made good. For all her fame, money, and worldly experience, Nita Hicks had to understand the faith of the people who tuned in to watch her every night. Their shared faith earned her their trust. She was one of them and acted as their eyes and ears when she told them what was happening in the world around them. Their pride boosted her ratings. But that was all in the producer's head. Nita Hicks was lost in the story – she never noticed that the red light on camera two had turned on.

Angela's aunt was building up to a furious explosion. In a decent world, her niece would not have ended up on life support. In a decent world, the apartment complex where they lived would have been adequately maintained. You could be sure that when people on Park Avenue complained that their elevator wasn't working right, it wouldn't take weeks for someone to come and check it out. Angela's aunt had checked the inspection slip that was posted in the stainless steel frame in the cab. The last time the city had tested the elevator had been in 1992. No one had looked at it in four years. Nobody cared about the people in their neighborhood. Somebody would have to pay.

'We're gonna sue the landlord himself. Personally.'

Angela's mother wasn't listening to her sister. She was trapped in the memories of her daughter. 'She used to want, she used to talk about wanting one of them Power Ranger dolls for her birthday.'

Angela's aunt's rage was unstoppable. 'We're gonna sue the housing authority. We're gonna sue the city. We're gonna sue Giuliani, Pataki, even damn President Clinton.'

Angela's mother was lost in the girl's dreams of magical transformations. Angela had been only eight years old but she knew that there was something better in the world than what she had.

'Regular people one minute, superheroes the next. The pink Ranger's the girl. Angie had her eye on the pink one. But now I dunno.'

Girl 6 remembered how much she had wanted a Barbie when she was little. She had hated third grade when Sean and Colleen Coughlin began calling her names. Girl 6 had begun staying in her room after school, just sitting and staring at Barbie – wishing she could be just like her. Barbie was blond. Movie stars were blond. Ballet dancers were blond. Everybody who was anybody was blond. Girl 6 hated who she was.

Things didn't get any better when she told her brother about the Coughlins. He had beaten the shit out of Sean even though her brother was a year younger and a couple of inches shorter. Girl 6 had never seen her father so mad. It wasn't that he was angry with his son: he was furious that his son and daughter already had to put up with this sort of shit. Girl 6 had never heard her father swear before, and when he calmed down he told her that there were a lot of Sean Coughlins in the world. Later, he had gone to see Sean's father and had come back even angrier than before. Sean was just a reflection of his father's racism. The neighborhood didn't welcome that kind of attitude, however, and the Coughlins moved the following year to whiter pastures.

'What my sister is saying is that this should not have happened. We're suing the system.' Angela's aunt was beginning to calm down after blowing off some steam.

Angela's mother was suddenly angry and confused. The press had made her family out to be something that it wasn't. The media had made certain assumptions – perhaps looking to improve their storyline, portraying Angela as a helpless kid struck down by a callous power structure.

'I got a job. My husband has jobs. I don't know why the papers wrote what they wrote. We're not on welfare.'

It was time to go back to the newsroom so Nita Hicks wrapped up the interview. 'We've been visiting with the mother and aunt of little Angela King. Up until yesterday the child was making a miraculous recovery, but now Little Angela King is back on the critical list here at Manhattan's Mount Sinai Hospital – we ask our viewers to send your prayers. I'm Nita Hicks reporting live from Mount Sinai Hospital. Back to you, Jim.' In the West Side television studio Jim Cowden looked seriously at the monitor before turning to his own camera. As earnestly as possible he replied, 'Thanks, Nita. We sure will.'

# CHAPTER SEVENTEEN

Girl 6 sat in her cubicle and juggled a number of calls.

'What's his name?'

'King. And he's a Great Dane. I want you to say hello to King.' Caller 17 was proud of his new dog.

'And I want you to show him your snatch.'

Girl 6 wasn't sure how to respond. What did Caller 17 want to hear from her? How was she supposed to feel about exposing herself to a large dog? She took a shot – what the hell.

'I'm nervous.'

The office was as busy as Girl 6 had ever seen it. She couldn't figure out why every guy in America was calling that night. Holidays were busy times but sometimes there was just no explanation for how things turned out.

Girl 6 switched the phone receiver up and flipped through her caller background cards. As Caller 17 savored her nervousness, Girl 6 was looking for David from Sarasota.

Caller 17 tried half-heartedly to ease her fear – but he didn't try too hard. He got off on the anxiety in Girl 6's voice.

'There's nothing to be afraid of. King is a good boy. Aren't you, King? King is saying yes. He's wagging his tail in the "yes" direction.'

Girl 6 found David from Sarasota – he was scared of girls and loved baseball. 'Approaching a girl is like approaching home plate, David.'

David from Sarasota, also known as Caller 18, sat in his thin-walled apartment wearing a jockstrap, cleats and a pair of batting gloves. Girl 6 spoke to him, playing him expertly.

'Sure, you're nervous. But you're no scrub. Have you got your hitter's eye on?'

Caller 18 fondled his Louisville Slugger and told Girl 6 that he was in the batter's box. 'I can see.'

Girl 6 knew that he was ready to play ball. 'I'm winding up with the pitch.'

As Caller 18 took his swings, Girl 6 flipped up Caller 18's receiver and flipped down Caller 17's. Some of the women had trouble balancing concurrent calls, but it came naturally to Girl 6. Caller 17 didn't even realize she had been gone as Girl 6 prepared to entertain his Great Dane.

'Okay, I'm relaxed now. Hi there, King. Look, here's my nice wet, hot, pink, juicy snatch.'

In the next cubicle Girl 19 played solitaire while she and Girl 4 did a double with Caller 21. 'You were swell to take us out after the game, Mark. Grab our butts like you grab a six pack of Bud.'

Lil surveyed the business from her office. Everyone was busy. Everyone was happy. Lil enjoyed the busy hum of the girls' conversations filling the room. Every now and then Lil let herself believe that her company contributed something beneficial to society. Think of all the unhappy men who found some sort of release for their frustrations. God only knew what some of these guys would be doing if they couldn't get their rocks off with her girls over the phone. They'd be out doing horrible things to desperate women. Lil was in one of her elevated moods that night and even began to dream about how much she actually helped her girls. It wasn't just the money. That was too obvious. They needed her cash to stay afloat and pursue whatever fanciful aspirations they had. But these were the women who would get hurt by men like some of her clients. These women were on the edge and vulnerable. She not only put roofs over their heads and food in their kitchens, she also protected them from the night-stalkers who might otherwise be hunting them in bars and on street corners. Lil's train of thought stalled. She couldn't allow that her clients were sick men – the great majority weren't, most were perfectly normal, or at least fairly normal. Most were just lonely or bored guys. Nobody in her line of work got hurt. That made her feel a lot better and she settled back in her chair to hear the girls talking and felt good about herself.

In the next room, Salesgirl 3 was cleaning a bank of telephones and untangling wires. Salesgirl 2 tallied phone minutes and waited for a new call to come in. 'They're busting their balls out there and it's quiet in here.'

That was fine with Salesgirl 3. 'I'm not complaining.' Salesgirl 3's mind was somewhere else. 'That girl Angela's gonna die, betcha.'

'Thanks a lot.' Salesgirl 2 didn't particularly like Salesgirl 3 and this just confirmed her worst thoughts.

Salesgirl 3 sprayed some Windex on to a phone and wiped with a Brawny paper towel. 'C'mon. I don't know why 6 and everybody else is tripping. It's not like she's related to the little girl. I feel for her too, but when your number is up, it's up.'

Salesgirl 2 didn't feel the need to be nice and polite any longer. 'You believe that shit?'

Salesgirl 3 unplugged a phone and let the receiver dangle – it spun quickly as the kinks came undone. 'Hell, yeah. Fate, the gods, whatnot. Somebody, something, said it's her turn, fair or not and she flew down the elevator shaft. It's the natural order of things.'

Salesgirl 2 had grown up in the church and left it after high school. Prayer seemed pretty weak in comparison to the forces on the street. Still, she couldn't accept Salesgirl 3's cynicism. 'You got a cold heart, sister.'

Salesgirl 3 plugged the phone back in. 'The world is cold.'

The phone rang immediately and she picked it up. 'Good evening, you're not going to be charged for talking with me. Can I have your name? Last name first. Norfleet, George. Can I have your address? Your billing address?'

Caller 9 stood naked in front of the picture window and looked down at the nation's capital. Snow and sleet were falling and the large window was drafty. Caller 9 had cranked up the heat, and as he listened to Girl 39 he touched his own flabby body. 'It hurts Black Mistress Tina.'

'It's supposed to hurt. Do it now, slave.' Girl 39 was pitiless as she turned the pages of *Rolling Stone*.

Caller 9 did as he was told. 'Your wish is my command, Black Mistress Tina.'

Girl 39 paused for a moment, noticing an article on the Wild Colonials. She loved their first disc and wished they'd tour to New York. Their music was exactly the sort of sound she hoped to play as a star in her own right someday. Girl 39 hesitated as she confused fantasies – for a moment she couldn't find her way and was lost between Caller 9's S&M aspirations and her own dreams of appearing at downtown clubs like The Cooler and the Mercury Lounge.

Girl 39 pulled herself together. She didn't want to piss off Caller 9. He'd paid a lot of her bills. 'Let's hear you count up to ten, slave. Opening and closing that nipple clip on your right one good and hard. With each count, degrade yourself or praise me, you follow?'

Caller 9 followed. Girl 39 remembered that Gods and Monsters were playing over the weekend and her bass-playing boyfriend was supposed to have gotten them on the comp list. She would have to remember to remind him.

'One: I'm a dumb fuck. Two: Oh, Mistress Tina, I wanna be your sex slave. Three: No one wants to fuck me. Four: I'm just your little dumb fuck slave.'

Shit. Her oldest niece was coming into town for an overnight sleepover and Girl 39 had forgotten to buy sheets for the fold-out bed in the living room. She made another mental note.

Every now and then, when things were either incredibly busy or Lil was just feeling nostalgic for the days when she opened her business as a one-woman outfit, she would come out of her office and would work the phones. When new women saw her sexing up guys they couldn't believe it. Lil was great at her job even though she didn't look the part. The new women quickly realized that they should pay attention to her dialogue. Lil was a master and there was a great deal they could learn from her.

Caller 25 was in crisis somewhere in West Hollywood. It was a good thing he was talking to Lil. Someone less experienced, less caring, might not have been able to talk him through the dark time. Lil blew the cigarette smoke out through her nose and commiserated.

'I've got eight healthy inches.'

On the West Coast, Caller 25 saw hope where he hadn't seen any previously. 'And you pass?'

Lil knew this was no time for elaborate bullshit. She gave a short and strong answer. 'Yes I do.' There was no doubt in her voice, no quavering.

Caller 25 couldn't miss her grit. 'I've been – I dunno. Sitting on the fence you could say about this for years.'

Lil wanted him to feel normal because she knew that was what he was desperate to feel. 'It's not for everybody. It's certainly not for me. I've got the best of both worlds.'

Lil rolled her eyes and sucked in some delicious nicotine. She was treating Caller 25 like he was white bread or a Ford fucking Taurus. How much more 'normal' could she make this sort of call? Christ. She was playing a happy semi-transsexual encouraging some confused son of a bitch to get it cut off. He wasn't Beaver Cleaver. He wasn't Richie Cunningham. He should have at least that much self-awareness. What the hell more did he want from her? Did he want the Pope to give his blessing from the balcony at the Vatican? Lil's stomach twisted when she thought about what her god-fearing mother would have thought about her little girl's career.

Lil covered the phone's mouthpiece as Girl 42 got carried away in the next cubicle. 'Oh, yeah, baby, please fuck me, fuck me, honey, yeah, do it, do it, ram me please . . .' Lil snapped her fingers for silence. Girl 42 was going too far – this wasn't a fucking circus – they would have to have a little talk during a break. Girl 42 scaled back her performance as directed.

Caller 25 hadn't heard a thing. He still sought reassurance. 'Could you send me a picture of yourself?'

A frigid rain fell on Manhattan and discouraged most people from going out. As fog settled down over the decaying West Side wharfs, Caller 30 walked out of a flop house and found a pay phone near Eleventh Avenue. When he walked out of his building it was still possible to see the lights of New Jersey across the Hudson River. In the time it took for Caller 30 to walk a few steps, all signs of life across the water vanished. Caller 30 stood in a dead neighborhood and made his nightly call. This time he was going to call someone new.

It was well past midnight and the phones had quietened down. Lil had gone home to Brooklyn having made a note to send a picture of Girl 4 to Caller 25. Girl 6 and a few other women worked the phones. Soda cans, plastic junk-food bags, cigarette butts, ash and empty cigarette packs littered the sex room. The place was trashed – it had been a great night. The janitor, who still had three hours of sleep to go before his alarm went off, had a lot of work ahead of him. When he arrived at the office later on, he was going to wish that he had stayed in bed.

Girl 6 was thinking of taking a break when Caller 30 was patched through to her. She wished she had left her station. Girl 6 could tell an asshole almost as soon as he got on the phone. The malice in Caller 30's voice was instantly recognizable. Girl 6 thought of hanging up, but reconsidered, realizing the man could pose no real threat to her. He had no idea where her office was. He had no idea where she lived. He had no idea what her real name was. Girl 6 was safe. She was there to make money and wasn't about to be faint-hearted now. Still, she had a bad feeling about Caller 30. She was going to earn her salary with this guy.

He certainly wasn't into small talk. 'Tell me you're a little wet slut.'

'I'm a little wet slut.' Give them what they want. That was her job.

Caller 30 paused. He seemed to get off on his next words. 'And you need to be put in this garbage bag.'

Girl 6 had never talked with anyone like Caller 30 before. She thought she could detour him away from the direction he was heading in. 'Let's talk.'

Caller 30 was focused. He wouldn't let Girl 6 change the subject. 'Nope. We can't talk 'cause I've gagged you. I've gagged you, you wet slut. Your hands are behind your back and now I'm mounting you. Ya silly head's in the big green baggie.'

Girl 6 was now scared – maybe this was a bad practical joke, maybe it was someone she knew. 'What's ya name, baby? Who is this?'

Caller 30 heard the fear in Girl 6's voice. He had found the girl of his dreams. 'I'm the love of ya life, bitch.'

Girl 6 hung up. It was over. He was gone. Caller 30 knew nothing about her other than the 900 number. He was a sick fuck passing in the night. Girl 6 stood, looked around the room, and was comforted by the familiarity of the women talking into their phones.

Girl 6 didn't leave work until the next afternoon. A line of her co-workers streamed out of the office building and made their ways home. Across the street the shoplifter kept an eye on them. Girl 6 was the last woman to leave and she started uptown. The shoplifter jogged through traffic and caught up with her. He wasn't sure what to say and he would kick himself later for the lame ice-breaker that he used.

'Working?'

Girl 6 was surprised to see him. At least she didn't tell him to fuck off. That was something.

The shoplifter tried again. 'Saw you walk in. Figured you had to come out sometime.'

Girl 6 couldn't figure out how many hours she had just spent on the job. She only knew that it was too many. She had to laugh at the shoplifter's suggestion that he had spent the night waiting for her. 'Didn't know you had a brain.' She was talked out. She didn't want to talk with the shoplifter. She didn't want to talk with anyone. She wanted to be left alone.

Girl 6 stopped walking and waited for the shoplifter to go on his way, but the shoplifter had nowhere to go other than to follow Girl 6. That's why he was there. That's what he had planned for the day. And so that was what he intended to do. The two of them stood awkwardly on the street corner. Silence. The shoplifter was growing increasingly uncomfortable and had to say something. 'Got anybody new?' Not exactly a light topic but it had been on his mind.

Girl 6 really didn't want to have this conversation. Even under the best of circumstances she wouldn't have wanted to have this conversation. But at the end of a seemingly endless shift – was it twelve hours, fourteen, sixteen . . . Girl 6 couldn't keep track – on a busy street, in cold weather, Girl 6 wanted no part of it. What was wrong with this guy? Didn't he get it? Girl 6 figured she would cut the conversation short before it really had a chance to begin.

'Yeah. His name's Bob Regular. He's great.'

The shoplifter was confused. What sort of name was Bob fucking Regular? What was the problem with Girl 6? Why was she always giving him a hard time? Girl 6 enjoyed the uncertain look on the shoplifter's face. He had no idea what she was talking about. Girl 6 wasn't entirely sure either. Bob Regular's name hadn't just been the luck of the draw. She hadn't said Caller 7's name or Caller 14's name. Bob Regular's name was in her mind. It had been looming there taking up space. She had been thinking about him. His name bursting out of her mouth was a confession that Girl 6 actually did have feelings for Bob Regular.

Girl 6 almost laughed when the shoplifter asked the obvious question. 'What kinda name is that?'

Girl 6 wasn't in the mood to draw him a map. 'I gotta run.'

The shoplifter might not have understood what was going on but he wasn't about to quit either. 'You eat?'

'I eat.'

The shoplifter wanted to buy her lunch. 'Let's . . .'

Girl 6 wasn't interested in the invitation, 'Not today. I've got other plans. Some other time.'

'Tomorrow?' The shoplifter wouldn't take a blow off.

Girl 6 looked at him blankly – he really didn't get it did he?

The shoplifter persisted. 'Friday? Aaaah, you like that, huh? Friday?'

'Fine.' Anything to shut him up. Anything to get away from him now, this minute, as quickly as possible.

It didn't take a lot to make the shoplifter happy. He knew that Girl 6 would keep her word even if she had given it ungenerously. He winked at her and smiled as he walked away backwards.

# CHAPTER EIGHTEEN

Girl 6 lay in her bath and read her fan mail. She had never received fan mail before. Even if it was from fucked-up guys it was still a new experience. In the background her tape machine played a Sarah Vaughan recording. How many people got letters from admirers? – and not just from one guy. Girl 6 was increasingly popular and got quite a few. With a slight adjustment of reality, Girl 6 was able to feel like a rising star, like she was someone who mattered, like she was arriving – even if she hadn't yet entirely made it.

Girl 6 looked at two photographs, giggled, and read a handprinted letter. Richard was a dentist. In one of the enclosed photographs he was standing in full medical uniform in his office. Richard looked like he had never been laid. Truth be told, Richard looked like he had never had a date. Richard was the nerd of nerds. The closest he had ever been to a woman was when he leaned over them while working on their mouths. Girl 6 read his letter to her.

Dear Miss Lovely,

Maybe you remember me. We spoke on Valentine's Day. I called you from Kansas City where I am gainfully employed as a dentist. Perhaps you remember. I very much wanted to meet you somehow – but as it seems meetings are against the rules, I am including a photograph of my groin area and a copy of my most recent tax return. Perhaps you will reconsider? In any case please send me your photograph.

Loads of love, Richard.

Girl 6 looked again at the second photograph. Unreal. What a moron this guy was. Richard the respectable dentist from Kansas City, Missouri, had sent Girl 6 a picture of his erect penis. After laughing for a few minutes, Girl 6 glanced at his tax forms. She was no accountant but she was certainly more impressed with his W2 and 1040 forms than with his dick.

Girl 6 dropped Richard to the floor. She picked up another piece of fan mail. Fan 2 was a bike messenger. She could see him standing on a sidewalk near Wall Street. Fan 2 was a skinny, fast-talking guy from Brooklyn. Fan 2 probably had a girlfriend but just got off talking dirty to anonymous women on the phone. He liked to hear things that his Jehovah's Witness girlfriend would never say. If Richard was dead serious and madly in love, Fan 2 was just amazed by the things that came out of Girl 6's mouth. He thought she was hilarious and looked forward to calling her blond bimbo character three times a week. 'Brigitte, I gotta tell you that you make me come fast! This is no small feat as I have had great hardness (ha ha) in coming at all ever since my lady . . .'

Boring. Fan 2 wasn't nearly as funny as he thought he was. Girl 6 knew a million guys like him. No one laughed at their jokes better than they did. Girl 6 let him slip to the puddle-covered floor and opened Fan 3's letter. Fan 3 was a New York City mounted cop. Fan 3 lived on Staten Island with four kids and a devoutly Catholic wife. One of his brothers worked for a cellular-phone service and got Fan 3 an amazing deal. Fan 3 could never have made the calls from his own home. His wife and their parish priest would have threatened him with excommunication and an eternity in hell if they ever knew. But with the new cell-phone he could call his favorite girl – Girl 6 – from anywhere, even from the saddle, which of course featured largely in the fantasies that Girl 6 spun for him. Fan 3 looked like a lot of tough, mid-thirties Irish guys. He was big, he knew how to fight – but he didn't look con-vincingly mean. Fan 3 was a good cop and also a likable guy. He didn't have an unfriendly bone in his body. Everybody –

his family, his neighbors, the people he patrolled, and even the people he caught – couldn't help but like him. Girl 6 was no different. Only she thought he should take the money he spent on her and use it for a good shrink. Girl 6 turned on the hot-water tap with her toes. She imagined Fan 3 sitting on top of his faithful horse Bullet somewhere in Central Park amidst the yuppies and the nannies as he re-read his letter to her, '. . . over my cock, Mistress April. Here's fifty bucks which should cover the cost and mailing of your panties. Soiled, please, if you don't mind, please. P.S. Wrap 'em in a plastic, zip-locked baggie enclosed for said purpose, as to ensure the strength of fragrance upon arrival.'

Girl 6 couldn't stop laughing and lowered herself beneath the surface of the hot water to calm down.

Later on, Girl 6 was still laughing as she sat in front of her vanity mirror. Her tape recorder played the cassette she borrowed from Girl 39. Girl 39's voice spoke in an exaggerated approximation of a French accent. 'My breasts are very large, forty-two double D. And I like them sucked. Ooooh. Suck my big breasts, big boy.'

As Girl 6 listened to the tape and practiced her own French accent, she put the finishing touches on a Cleopatra Jones look. Girl 6 looked at herself with approval. She was the very image of the 1970s, Black action chick. Girl 6 wore a big afro with a golden head sash, blue eyeliner, colorful mod blouse and a fake gunbelt.

Girl 6 repeated after Girl 39. 'My breasts are very large. Forty-two double D. And I like them sucked. Oooh, suck my big breasts, big boy.'

Girl 6's eyes stared briefly at two pictures that had been added to her collection of women taped to her wall. The photographs had been ripped from newspapers. One showed Angela King as a happy child, playing with her mother and father underneath a Christmas tree. Girl 6 saw intelligence, warmth and good humor in the little girl's eyes. Angela clearly had potential to live a fulfilling life. She had what it took, and not everyone did. Girl 6 couldn't believe that Angela had been robbed of those gifts. Girl 6 couldn't believe that Angela might die or be left without a mind. Girl 6 looked at a second picture that showed Angela lying unconscious in Mount Sinai's Intensive Care Unit. It was too terrible to think about so Girl 6 decided not to.

Instead, she rewound the tape and played it again as the payphone in the hallway started to ring. Girl 39 repeated herself, '. . . ooh. Suck my big breasts, big boy.'

Girl 6 shifted back to her good mood. 'Ooo la la, suck Brigitte's big titties, big all-American boy.'

The phone in the hallway continued to ring.

*Girl 6 as Cleopatra Jones – the once-supreme queen of Black exploitation films – listened to a pink princess dial-phone as it rang in her psychedelic seventies apartment. Girl 6 as Cleopatra Jones was the total image of the super-mod soul sister, from her afro to her platform boots. Girl 6 as Cleopatra Jones spoke with a fearless speed into the phone, 'Talk to me fast, baby, 'cause I got five heavy-tripping jive turkeys on my tail.'*

*A voice that sounded an awful lot like Jimmy from next door spoke back to her. 'Chief wants us to join him in Paris. There's a 4:30 plane. I'm just across town, I'll come pick you up.'*

*That was fine with Girl 6. 'I'm here baby.'*

*The voice on the other end of the phone signed off, 'Stay Black and beautiful, sister.'*

*Girl 6 put her fist in the air. 'Right on! Power to the people.'*

*Girl 6 spun around as the shoplifter as Bad Guy 1 appeared in the room behind her. 'Put down the phone, lady. You're surrounded.'*

*Somewhere off the movie screen of her mind, Jimmy as Girl 6's co-agent, asked frantically, 'What's wrong? Who's there? I'll be right over.'*

*Girl 6 as the Mod Sister didn't need anybody's help. She checked out the situation – Girl 6 was surrounded by the shoplifter and four gigantic Black guys all wearing dark turtlenecks. They looked bad. But as bad as they were, they were no match for Girl 6. A series of karate chops and a few well-placed kicks knocked all the bad guys into submission. Before losing consciousness a battered and bruised shoplifter as Bad Guy 1 moaned, 'Damn, woman. Who the hell are you?'*

*The door flew open and Jimmy as Girl 6's co-agent rushed into the room with his gun drawn. He was too late – there was nothing left for him to do. Jimmy as the secret agent was impressed. 'Damn, woman you a bad . . .'*

*A tinny chorus belted out a song from the soundtrack in Girl 6's mind. 'Shut your mouth.'*

*Jimmy smiled and gave the camera a goofy look of admiration. 'I'm just talking about Mod Sister.'*

*The Lovely Brown theme-music pumped up into its full soul glory and Girl 6 as the Mod Sister stood looking at the camera with a defiant hand on her hip. Girl 6 flipped open a special wallet to reveal a special intelligence agency ID card. The camera in Girl 6's mind pushed in and showed the presidential seal and Girl 6's photograph. Underneath her face was printed in cheesey looking seventies computer font – Special Agent to the President: Lovely Brown. Credits rolled and 'GIRL 6 as LOVELY BROWN in MOD SISTER' titles swirled across Girl 6's imagination.*

The payphone in the hallway outside continued to ring. No one had bothered to pick it up. Certainly Jimmy wasn't going to do it. Girl 6 was pulled back into the here and now by its nagging ring. She ran outside in full Mod Sister costume and picked up the receiver. For a moment she answered the phone as Lovely Brown Special Agent to the President – and then shook the last remnants of her fantasy from her mind. Girl 6 was herself again. A familiar voice said hello on the other end. 'It's Bob, Lovely.'

Was Girl 6 supposed to be Girl 6 or Lovely Brown? She decided upon a modified version of herself. Bob from Tucson – aka Caller 1 – called her Lovely, but in truth he knew the difference. He knew the girl he was talking to. After an instant's hesitation, Girl 6 found her role. 'Where ya been?' She'd been worried. Bob hadn't called for some time now.

'Busy. I thought you'd be happy.' He had detected something in Girl 6's voice that he wasn't familiar with. It might have been anger. It might have been unhappiness. Either way, it was something of a challenge and he wasn't used to it.

Girl 6 didn't realize that he had noticed the difference in her tone. She was genuinely pleased to hear from him. 'I am happy. It's just funny hearing your voice, that's all. How's your mom, dude?'

Bob didn't respond to the question. He had another agenda. 'Guess what? Tomorrow I'm in town for one day only to close a big deal. I've got some free time around two. Let's do something crazy.'

Girl 6 was surprised by the suggestion. To any other client she would have said no without giving it any further thought. Clients were money, money was her ticket out of New York, and she wasn't willing to jeopardize her relationship with a good client. It wasn't worth it. But in Bob's case, Girl 6 felt different. The only problem was that she was scheduled to be on the phones. 'I'm working a double shift tomorrow.'

Caller 1 was used to getting his own way with Lovely. He didn't expect to be contradicted. He didn't like to hear 'no.' Bob from Tucson tried some charm. 'Coney Island for a hot dog. And then we'll make love under the boardwalk. Just like the song.'

Girl 6 didn't know what to say. It was a lot easier to suck him, fuck him, whatever him over the phone than to make an arrangement for a more traditional date. Facts were facts. 'I'm working.'

Bob from Tucson didn't accept no for an answer. He was too used to getting exactly what he wanted. 'Take a vacation.

Two p.m. I've missed you, girl. Chance of a lifetime! Say it's a date. Come on . . .'

Girl 6 was torn. She hated the idea of missing a shift, but Bob was different from the other guys. She answered warily, 'One hot dog, that's all, nothing else.'

# CHAPTER NINETEEN

Coney Island in winter was pretty much deserted. It was a gray, dreary, damp, day and everything that Girl 6 looked at was depressing. She thought there was nothing more discouraging than a place that was designed for crowds of people having fun when it was empty and abandoned. The snack bars, the signs luring people into different attractions, the wild rides, the noble Wonderwheel were all spattered with a slushy rain and grimly silent. They were there to provide fun for the pleasure-seeking people who came to Coney Island, but summer was long gone and the crowds had rejected them for warmer, more interior entertainments. Coney Island looked forsaken – a hulking, soggy, steel and neon bride left standing forlornly at the altar.

Despite the gloomy surroundings, the atmosphere didn't bring Girl 6 down. Her mood was impregnable. Girl 6 sat on a bench and looked around happily as though it were a warm spring evening and she was scoping the passing crowds. Girl 6 had dressed up and was wearing her version of a Sophia Loren outfit – a small, simple dress that showed plenty of shoulder, breast and leg. The material was a single vivid color without patterns. It was simple, elegant and sensual. Girl 6 had accentuated her eyebrows and wore a bold red lipstick. Her hair was a wig that was reminiscent of the sixties but not too much so. She looked great – too great for Coney Island. Maybe even too great for the real world. Yet she didn't look like a freak, or like someone who was trying too hard. Girl 6 knew she could carry it off and she didn't want to disappoint her favorite caller. She had existed in his mind as a figure of fantasy and Girl 6 was determined to live up to his expectations. If she were honest with herself she would have admitted that they were her expectations too. By assuming the look she became everything that it suggested.

The only acknowledgement she made to the phone-sex office – the foundation of their relationship – was a golden name pin which spelled out 'Lovely' in swirly cursive script. It was pinned on her dress and clearly visible through her open coat. Before she arrived, she thought she needed some identification – how else would Bob be able to pick her out of the crowd? But there were few enough people on the boardwalk today – and unless Bob from Tucson was expecting her to be a bent-over, old man with hair growing out of his nose and ears, he would have no problem recognizing her.

After an hour had passed, Girl 6 started to feel the chill. Bob from Tucson was going to be late. Maybe his flight was delayed because of bad weather somewhere. Girl 6 took the 'Lovely' pin off her dress, pinned it to her lapel, and buttoned the coat shut. She had been thinking about a Nathan's hot dog ever since Bob from Tucson had mentioned it. Girl 6 would have preferred to eat with Bob when he arrived, but she hadn't eaten anything all day – she'd wanted to be really hungry when it came time to eat. By three o'clock, Girl 6's hunger had become painful. If Bob from Tucson wanted to eat when he finally arrived, that would be fine. Girl 6 couldn't wait any longer. Besides, the food would help her fight the chill.

The guy at Nathan's seemed almost as happy to see Girl 6 as she was to see him. During the frantic summer months he had dreamed about the quiet, peaceful winter days. Now that he was there, he wasn't so thrilled. He was bored. The place was melancholy and desolate. When Girl 6 walked up to his counter and ordered, the man began talking as he put together the best hot dog he could assemble. He always liked showing off for a pretty girl, and this lady was a knockout. He was disappointed, however, when all Girl 6 wanted was a dog with mustard and relish. He was hurt when she didn't want to talk. He watched her walk away and figured she was some stuck-up bitch who didn't want to pass the time with a guy who was a hot dog chef. Maybe when he got home that night he'd call Monique. She was expensive, but

114

she was always thrilled to hear from him and talked as long as he wanted. Thinking about their last conversation, he squeezed a jar of mustard too hard and its contents spurted out the top, staining his uniform. It was a hell of a life.

After the hot dog, Girl 6 got bored waiting. She went to buy a ticket for the Wonderwheel from its sleepy manager. He was taking a nap and when he woke up to find Girl 6 standing in front of him, the man thought he was dreaming. Something about this young girl reminded him of when he'd been stationed in Palermo after the war. It didn't make sense to him – this was 1996 and the girl was Black. The manager smiled and decided not to bother to try and work it through. Sometimes you just accepted the gifts that the good lord sent to you. He wouldn't take her money. Girl 6 rode the massive Wonderwheel all by herself. The vacant carriages around her bobbed and rattled emptily as the bleak city lay lifelessly beneath her. Girl 6 felt desperately alone.

Afterwards, Girl 6 walked around looking for Bob from Tucson. She bought a ticket for the Cyclone and rode it by herself.

Several hours later, Girl 6 sat alone on the boardwalk, a solitary figure. There was no sign of Bob. Although she had a sense of unease, Girl 6 was determined not to give up. How could someone stand her up like this? How could someone stand up Girl 6 as Sophia Loren? It just didn't happen. Not to a woman like that. Not to a woman like her.

Late afternoon closed in and night began to fall. Girl 6 crouched at the edge of the water and built a sand castle. She had plenty of time and put a lot of care into its construction. It was a beautiful sand castle, elaborately designed, with turrets and a drawbridge made from a Yoo-Hoo container. As the tide rolled in, Girl 6 walked back towards the boardwalk and watched as the waves tore her creation apart.

It was dark and Girl 6 had retreated back to her bench on the boardwalk. Bob from Tucson had blown her off. She'd give it another few minutes. Another few passers by, and she would call it a day.

Girl 6's eyes shut for a few minutes. When she woke up she spotted a man walking towards her. She had been dreaming about Caller 1 and when she saw someone approaching, she assumed it was her long-delayed lover.

'Bob Regular?'

The man looked at Girl 6 as though she were crazy and walked a little faster, quickly disappearing into the shadows.

Girl 6 gave up and rode the subway home. There was no one else on the train. Girl 6 sat alone as she was buffeted by the lurching car. She looked up at the small billboard advertising: 'Dental Bonding – Be the New You,' 'Meet the Love of Your Life – Call the Relationship Line,' 'Be Everything You Want to Be – Join the Better You Fitness Club!' Girl 6 had been thinking of joining a gym. She had enough cash coming in. She spotted a little tear-off sheet that contained an introductory discount coupon. Girl 6 decided to join. Girl 6 decided to take the tear-off sheet. But she couldn't move. She couldn't get up off the subway car's seat. Girl 6 was stuck where she was – paralyzed, exhausted. She was rejected and dejected, deflated and frustrated.

Arriving back at the New Amsterdam Royal, Girl 6 walked down the hallway to her apartment. Instead of going inside and taking a bath as she had intended, Girl 6 stopped at Jimmy's door. There were reasons for failure. Maybe there was a good reason for why Bob from Tucson hadn't shown up. Maybe she wasn't as good at what she did as she thought she was. There was more she could do to improve herself. There had to be something more she could do to make Bob from Tucson really like her, more she could do to make him do what he said he would – like not let her down.

Girl 6 knocked on the door. No answer. She knocked again and this time Jimmy opened the door. He stared at Girl 6 coldly, not particularly happy to see her. Girl 6 asked if she could come

116

in. He didn't exactly invite her inside but Jimmy opened the door wider.

Jimmy's apartment looked the same as always. She saw copies of the different local daily papers scattered on a table. The sports sections had been pulled out and read thoroughly. They were strewn across the room. The remainder of the papers hadn't been touched.

Jimmy didn't say anything. He didn't know what the deal was with Girl 6, so he shrugged. Girl 6 teased him.

'Don't be so excited to see me.'

Jimmy knew Girl 6 wasn't there to see him. She was there because she wanted to talk to him about someone else. Fuck that. It wasn't his job to talk to people about what was bothering them – that was her job. She could talk to herself if she really needed to and provide her own therapy. Girl 6 was usually all business with him so Jimmy was determined to be all business with her. 'What can I do for you?'

Girl 6 hadn't expected his attitude. Jimmy had always been thrilled to see her. She knew he listened to the noises from the hallway. She knew he recognized the sound of her footsteps. She knew that they didn't just accidentally run into each other in the hall. Girl 6 would have been more than happy to see a man excited by her appearance at this moment. In fact, she had counted on Jimmy's reaction and was disappointed. Still, she wasn't the type to give up.

'C'mon Jimmy, I had a hard day, got stood up by Bob from Tucson.'

'What did ya expect?' Jimmy wasn't surprised. Girl 6 couldn't see straight nowadays. Who the fuck was Bob from Tucson to stand her up? Why couldn't she see that Jimmy from down the fucking hallway would never have stood her up? Jimmy was pissed that she didn't feel anything for him and pissed that she was acting so stupid about Bob.

Girl 6 didn't want Jimmy's shit right now. Girl 6 wanted him to open his door and be thrilled to see her. She made total strangers think she was thrilled to hear from them for two shifts a day. Why couldn't someone do that for her at least this one time, 'Why do you have to go there? I thought we were friends.'

Jimmy's resolve weakened. 'Me too.'

Girl 6 saw the opportunity to change the subject and dove into the reason for her visit. 'Good. I need a favor.' Jimmy held up his hands in self-defense. He liked Girl 6 but was in no position to do anybody favors. Before he could say no, Girl 6 continued her explanation.

'These guys call, they always want to talk about sports and I need to be more knowledgeable.'

This was a whole different thing to Jimmy. Girl 6, his Girl 6, the Girl 6 of his dreams wanted him to teach her about sports? She thought she was asking him for a favor? Jimmy laughed inside. Favors like that Jimmy could do any time. The prospect of combining sports with Girl 6 was Jimmy's idea of heaven. So what if she wanted this information so she could better sex up her callers. If Girl 6 spent time with Jimmy talking about sports she would see him for what he really was, fall in love with him, give up the phone job, and they'd live happily ever after. Jimmy was glad he hadn't sulked.

'Well, you've come to the right place, the right person. I got all types of books. For a nominal fee I could tutor you also. Let me give you the quickie crash course. Step into the shrine.'

Jimmy led Girl 6 into the adjoining room, which he called the Mini Sports Memorabilia Hall of Fame. This is where Jimmy's heart was. 'See these jerseys? Numbers 39, 36, and 42 all worn by what three Black players of the Brooklyn Dodgers?'

Girl 6 smiled warmly. 'I have no idea. I don't know.'

Jimmy was stunned. She was an educated woman, how could she not know? This was American history, this was her heritage. 'Whatdoyoumean you don't know. Take a guess.' Jimmy couldn't believe she really had no idea.

Girl 6 took a shot. 'Reggie Jackson?'

'Reggie Jackson! Jesus Christ. 36 is pitcher Don Newcombe,

118

39 is three-time MVP Hall of Famer Roy Campanella and number 42 is the first African American to play major league baseball in the modern era.'

'Jackie Robinson?' Girl 6 knew that much.

Jimmy was pleased she wasn't a complete idiot. He could work with her. 'If you missed that one I would have shot you.' She had passed a test of sorts. Maybe not with flying colors, but a minimal passing grade.

Girl 6 looked around the memorabilia room. Something about it struck her as familiar. She wasn't sure what it was. Poor Jimmy was trapped in here with the cast-off possessions of the men he wanted to be. When was he going to join the real world?

'What else you got? These are real things? They wore these?'

'Yep, the real McCoy, game used. Ewing's, Stark's, Mason's jerseys.' Jimmy was proud. These were the holy of holies. Jimmy pulled a pair of boxing gloves off a shelf. He slipped them on. They were several sizes too big for him. 'Mike Tyson's boxing gloves, knocked out Alex Stewart.' Jimmy slipped his bare feet into a gigantic pair of sneakers. He 'dribbled' around Girl 6, charged down the court in his mind and slam-dunked a phantom ball into his little Nerf-ball hoop stuck to a closet door with suction cups. 'Money's Air Jordans, wore these the night he got fifty-five on the Knicks.'

Girl 6 looked around the room. It was a pretty impressive collection for what it was. Jimmy ought to make some money with it now, instead of waiting twenty years for his cards to 'mature.'

'Sell some of this stuff.'

Jimmy hadn't ever, wouldn't ever, consider doing that. The trophies in this room meant much more to him than money. They were much more integral to his survival than the food that money could buy. They provided proximity and tangibility to his dreams. 'Never. But my newest acquisition is a whopper. Close your eyes.' Girl 6 did as she was told. Jimmy opened a box and pulled out a jock strap. 'Okay, open 'em.'

The jock strap was mammoth, and Girl 6 had trouble

recognizing it for what it was. When she realized just what she was seeing, Girl 6 tried to imagine how it could have any significance to a sane person. 'What is that?'

Jimmy was proud but Girl 6 was relieved to see that he wasn't taking himself – or his trophy – too seriously. 'This is Shaq Fu's jock strap that he wore in his rookie season. Want a sniff?' Before Girl 6 could answer, Jimmy pushed the fragrant supporter into her face like a crazed perfume salesman. Girl 6 lost it. She was screaming. Girl 6 and Jimmy laughed like they hadn't laughed in a long time.

# CHAPTER TWENTY

It was the end of a long day and Girl 6 hadn't wanted to leave the warmth of Jimmy's company, but she had an overnight shift to pull and Girl 6 found herself back at the phone-sex office all too soon, ready to begin again. As she walked in and picked up her log, Girl 6 overheard two of the saleswomen talking. 'She get that doll you sent?'

Salesgirl 1 had just received a thank-you note. 'Yeah. Along with like nine-thousand seven-hundred and something others.' Salesgirl 2 was happy to hear that. She felt vindicated – there were people in the world who cared. Individuals did make a difference. 'Little Angie's in the pink.'

Salesgirl 1 opened her desk drawer and showed Salesgirl 2 a handwritten letter. 'I got a thank-you note. From her aunt.' Salesgirl 1 read proudly, 'Dear Miss, thank you very much, sincerely, Aretha Green her auntie. P. S. Don't believe the hype.' Salesgirl 1 and 2 enjoyed a self-satisfied laugh.

As Girl 6 finished signing in and picking up her things, Lil addressed her without even looking up from her paperwork. 'You're late.' Girl 6 had never been late before. It was just like Lil not to cut her any slack. Girl 6 said nothing and went into the lounge.

A couple of women were sitting around talking and smoking. Girl 6 walked in and saw that there was a live report in progress from Mount Sinai's long-term convalescent facility. Girl 6 grabbed the earphones and plugged herself in. Reporter Nita Hicks sat by little Angela's bedside. 'Too often bringing you a late breaking story means that we have to put what was once an important story on a back burner; and sometimes that story is forgotten altogether. Four months ago we brought you the story of little Angela King's tragic accident. Not long after that,

121

Angela's mother made a birthday wish on her unconscious daughter's behalf – that people insist the responsible authorities ensure the safety of the city's children. Tonight we're following up with Angela accompanied by a very, very special guest.'

The camera panned from Hicks to the perfectly put-together face of the moment's most desirable movie star. She waited until the camera resolved upon her face, looked as sincere as she possibly could make herself appear to be, and spoke. 'I'm here because we're all here, Nita. Because Mrs King's birthday wish moved over eleven-thousand people to respond. And in this city, in this day and age, that's a modern miracle.'

Girl 6 unplugged herself. She had heard enough. What was this movie-star lady talking about? What had Nita Hicks just said? They said nothing. The words didn't add up to a single meaningful thought. Icing but no cake. They were vampires sustaining their careers with little Angela's blood. No doubt the star had a movie opening and the studio wanted to get her seen by as many people as they could. No doubt she had spent the morning with Regis and Cathie Lee, moved on to Dave in the late afternoon, and was now being seen with little Angela in time for the eleven o'clock news. No movie star, sports hero or television reporter had thought more about Angela King than Girl 6. The little girl's accident haunted her thoughts day and night. Movie stars broadcasting from the bedside of a comatose child? It made her sick. What was wrong with these people? Didn't they know what they really accomplished with their televised sympathy? It wasn't a harmless activity. They cheapened the tragedy with their exploitation of it. Dead babies and ratings didn't mix. Didn't they know words counted? Girl 6 couldn't believe they were so blind.

For all her anger, though, an image stuck in Girl 6's mind. The movie star at the little girl's bed. The magnificent and the pitiful. Even if the words the star spoke were meaningless, her appearance couldn't help but have significance to Girl 6, to the little girl, to the family, to the world. Someone as exalted and beauti-

122

ful as the movie star lady had cared. It was too bad that she had opened her mouth. Still, it was a moment that grew in Girl 6's imagination. Between the night's callers, Girl 6 thought more and more about what she had seen. Her anger at what she had imagined had been the star's mercenary motivation subsided. Gradually the strength of the imagery overwhelmed her cynical take on why the bedside visit had been arranged. During Girl 6's three a. m. break she went into the lounge and saw the pictures from the hospital on the re-broadcast of the evening's local news. She didn't bother to plug herself in this time. This way she would only see the beautiful woman sitting next to the stricken child, the divine and the mortal.

Tears came to Girl 6's eyes. She was moved by the movie star's willingness to interrupt her busy schedule for this small girl. Girl 6 felt that in some way she too had been personally visited – touched – by the great woman's presence. On some level, Girl 6 identified with little Angela King and felt rescued, uplifted. Girl 6 identified with the movie star – even if she hadn't reached the other woman's lofty position in the world yet. Girl 6 knew she too could bring the same balming assistance to Angela King and the other Angela Kings of the world. Maybe by assuming that role she would somehow make it true. It could be a transforming act.

Girl 6 was unusually unfocused when she returned to the phones. Salesgirl 1 already had a call waiting for her. The voice sounded familiar and Girl 6 began to concentrate, trying to place exactly who the caller was. It didn't take long for her to remember Caller 30's vicious fantasies.

'And then, I'd tie you down real good.'

Girl 6 wanted to keep him away from that sort of discussion. 'Have we talked before?' Caller 30 said they hadn't. Girl 6 remembered her hands being bound behind her back – remembered being suffocated in the green trash bag as he fucked her from behind. Girl 6 wanted to get a little more information about Caller 30 and then talk to Lil.

'What's your name, Sweetheart?'

123

'Jack Spratt. What's yours?'

Girl 6 wanted to keep him happy, keep him on the line, maybe he'd give something away about himself. 'Mrs Spratt. Lovely Spratt. Really.'

Caller 30 didn't buy it. 'Bullshit. Who are you?'

'Anybody you want, baby.'

Girl 6 learned all too well who Caller 30 wanted her to be.

'You ain't anybody. You ain't even nobody. You ain't even shit, bitch.'

Girl 6 was frozen by his contempt. She had never talked with anyone like this before. Girl 6 tried to respond when the call was disconnected. Instead of Caller 30, Girl 6 heard Lil's voice over the phone. She looked to her right and saw Lil looking directly at her from the office window. 'I cut him off, okay. You don't have to be polite.'

Girl 6 was still a little stunned by the events. 'I wasn't being polite.'

'Well, whatever, don't be it. Don't encourage them.' Lil hung up.

'Right,' Girl 6 agreed to an empty telephone line.

Girl 6's phone began to flash and beep. She plugged in and picked up. Caller 30 was back on the line. 'Why did you do that? Don't be shy, Girl 6. I just wanna talk. I'll be good. I'll be nice, okay?'

Girl 6 looked back at Lil's office. She was pouring over paperwork as usual. Girl 6 thought about hanging up. She thought about telling Lil, but she couldn't. She felt something new, something that took her by surprise. If she were honest with herself, though, maybe the feeling wasn't that new and wasn't that big of a surprise – maybe it was something she had known all along. Girl 6 found that she was both disgusted and fascinated by Caller 30. Girl 6 shrugged and rationalized that she needed the money and stayed on the line.

# CHAPTER TWENTY-ONE

The shoplifter waited outside the phone-sex office. He stood in a doorway to avoid the freezing wind and stomped his feet to stay warm. He looked at his watch. The shift was over – why wasn't Girl 6 coming downstairs? A flood of women had exited the building heading home for the night. The shoplifter shook his head. It was a crazy world. He didn't call phone-sex lines himself but had a basic idea of what they were all about. While he wasn't thrilled that this was how Girl 6 was making her money, he could understand it. You didn't always get the job you planned, but you had to survive somehow. The shoplifter, for example, hadn't spent his childhood dreaming about being a thief. He had wanted to be a musician – not a mega star, just a working musician. The shoplifter remembered looking out his bedroom window as a little kid and seeing a guy walking home at four in the morning carrying an instrument case. That seemed like the sort of life he wanted, walking alone in an empty city, living by your own rules, not working in some goddamn office and punching a clock at nine a.m., not taking shit from bosses. He remembered his father yelling to his mother about the asshole he worked for. The anger and frustration in his father's voice had terrified him. He couldn't imagine what could make his father sound like that. Whatever it was, he wanted no part of it. He wasn't going to lead his life that way. He wouldn't make that mistake. He would be his own man.

The shoplifter signed up for band class back in the days when public schools still had music programs and before Reagan declared ketchup a vegetable. His career ambitions took a serious hit, however, when he discovered that he had no musical talent. His teacher admired his heart and encouraged him. The young shoplifter tried half a dozen musical instruments before he realized that he couldn't make it. Years later, the shoplifter realized that what appealed to him about the lone jazz musician walking home late at night was the way the man led his life, not what he did.

The shoplifter also realized as an adult that a person tended to do what he did best. People tried different things, tried to control what they did, but generally speaking they fell into the area of their natural expertise. You found your place in the world. The shoplifter had started stealing small things as a kid and knew immediately that it was something he did well. After some time, the shoplifter knew also that it was something he had to do. It was compulsive. The shoplifter didn't hate anybody and didn't wish the storekeepers any ill will. On the contrary, he wished them well because then there'd be better stuff for him to take.

As the shoplifter waited outside the phone-sex office for Girl 6 he laughed quietly. He could imagine Girl 6 doing phone sex. If he were ever to call a 900 number he would want to talk to a woman who looked like Girl 6. Girl 6 was someone you could fantasize about. The shoplifter looked at some of the other phone-sex operators and couldn't believe it. If only the guys on the other end of the phone knew who they thought they were fucking. Before the shoplifter could finish that thought he had another more disturbing one. If people found their places in the world – if they did what they did best – what if this was what Girl 6 was supposed to be doing? What if this was what Girl 6 did best? The shoplifter had a few bad moments while he considered this possibility. Then he dismissed it. This was what Girl 6 was doing for the moment. This was how she paid her rent and prepared to take the next step. The shoplifter had faith in her. Girl 6 wouldn't let herself be sucked into believing that this was anything real.

The shoplifter thought it was pretty funny when some of the girls coming out of the phone-sex office eyed him suspiciously. What did they think he was thinking about? Chances were he couldn't imagine anything as wild as they talked about every day at work.

'Hi. Let's go.' The shoplifter was surprised to hear Girl 6's voice. She had walked up behind him.

'Where were you?'

Girl 6 was already walking down the street. 'This way. Come on. I don't wanna be seen with you.'

The shoplifter didn't know what had just happened. 'Damn.' He caught up with Girl 6 and they walked along, heading downtown. The shoplifter stole a look at her. They couldn't punish him for that. Girl 6's expression told him otherwise – maybe she could.

Girl 6 stared straight ahead, never making eye contact.

'I took the day off. I'll pick up some hours later.'

Girl 6 and the shoplifter sat in a diner with Formica-covered tables and worn naugahide booths. Both were eating pumpkin pie and drinking coffee. Girl 6 wasn't sure why she was sitting there. Girl 6 wasn't sure why she was even talking to the shoplifter, much less eating a meal with him, but she was there and she would make the best of it. The shoplifter hadn't said a word since his slice of pie arrived. He ate it quickly as though he expected someone to take it away from him at any moment. As he neared the crust he had eaten enough so that he could talk. 'You miss me?'

'No.' Girl 6 wasn't interested in a long evening with the shoplifter.

The shoplifter wasn't bothered by her taciturn reply. 'I miss you. How are you doing?'

'Fine, and yourself?' Girl 6 wasn't going to give him anything.

The shoplifter felt a need to talk to Girl 6. 'My usual criminal activity. I still haven't used a gun. Don't intend to. And I don't go into people's houses.'

Girl 6 finished her coffee. This wasn't news. The shoplifter wasn't the type of guy to hurt somebody. The shoplifter sometimes liked to talk about himself as though he were public enemy number one, as though he could barely hold himself back from shooting up the town, like he was only a little self-control away from being a crazed, violent gangster like Pacino in *Scarface*. Girl 6 sighed. Everyone had their dreams. The fact was, the shoplifter wasn't a bad person at all – unless you were a local merchant. The shoplifter was a petty thief and that's all he would ever be.

The shoplifter continued to fill her in with what was going on in his life. 'I take from those who've got more than they need. That's still my speed.'

Great. Girl 6 was thrilled to be having pie with the Robin Hood of Harlem. She looked him straight in the eye as he continued his talk.

'You know: supermarkets, the Woolworths. Macy's. Korean delis. Only take what I can use. Clothes, food. Your basic fruits and vegetables. Meats, chickens, beef, pork, coldcuts. Rice. Cereals. Milk.' The shoplifter noticed that Girl 6 was finally looking at him, finally acknowledging his existence. That was something. 'Damn, you're looking good. We had us some fun, huh? Yeah.'

Girl 6 didn't respond. A waiter came by and brought them more pumpkin pie.

The shoplifter swerved back compulsively to his talk. Girl 6 had been interested for a moment when he'd actually talked about something, talked about them, but now the bullshit was back. 'Thanks, man. I try to eat balanced. I still got my sweet tooth, but you know. I still got my bad habits. It only takes one thing you know. Could be anything. Any one thing to push me over.'

Girl 6 thought he was sad. When the shoplifter lived in reality, he was an all right guy. But he couldn't stay away from the big talk. He was off again, talking like some gangster trying to impress some hood rat chick.

'I gotta watch my step. One thing: push. Smack. Right over into Bad-land. Into Evil-city. Anything. Could be anything. Then I'd be like, you know, hanging up in a post office.'

The shoplifter laughed at the possibility. Girl 6 didn't. She was tired of all the crap and wanted to change the subject. 'How's everybody?'

The shoplifter followed her lead. 'Moms doesn't like me living at home. I told her I'd seen you, she said an ex-wife's a sign.'

Girl 6 let the waiter refill her cup and played it off. 'Brothers okay?'

The shoplifter didn't want to talk about his family, but if that's what Girl 6 wanted, he'd tell her. 'So far all right. Still hungry. I boosted a twenty-four-pound turkey for Moms this last Thanksgiving. She just put it in the oven, didn't ask me where it comes from, just slides it in the oven no questions asked. The brothers gotta eat.' The shoplifter laughed at his own story.

Girl 6 eased up a little and smiled. 'How's – uh what'shername? Miss Hot Stuff?'

The shoplifter tried to charm his way through that problem. 'Doreen – History, Her-story. You've always been my only true love, you know that.'

Girl 6 didn't want to hear it. 'I'm leaving as soon as I'm able. For good. California.'

The shoplifter didn't like the news, but didn't want to contradict her. 'Oh yeah! I've never been to California.'

Girl 6 had something inside her that she'd wanted to say for a while. She just hadn't known who to say it to. The shoplifter seemed like a good choice. If he had the stuff inside him that she thought he did, he would understand. If he didn't he'd just keep on talking, not notice, and it wouldn't matter.

'You ever start something for a certain reason then after you got started kinda forgot why you started but couldn't quit neither?'

She had actually said something to him – something important. The shoplifter's voice was quiet. 'Sometimes. When I'm boosting something. I always get caught when that happens.'

Girl 6 altered the conversation slightly. 'You been following that girl Angie in the news?'

129

The shoplifter didn't really follow the news except when he could slip a copy from a stand or convenience store. Still, everybody in town knew about Angela King. 'Yeah. That's messed up.'

Girl 6 didn't pursue the matter and soon they were talking about the shoplifter again. He went on about himself for another piece of pie and then figured it was time to find out exactly what Girl 6 was doing with herself. The shoplifter pretended he didn't know where she was working. 'You do that freelance typing thing, temp, right?'

Girl 6 didn't believe for a second that the shoplifter didn't know what she was doing. Even if he truly hadn't known though, she would have been completely up front, she had nothing to hide. 'Wrong. Phone sex.'

The shoplifter knew she knew but kept up the pretense. 'No shit. You?'

Girl 6 understood the shoplifter well enough to know that he was trying to be noble in his own way by pretending to be surprised. 'Why not me? You ever called one?'

The shoplifter had not, or so he said. 'Hell no. I like touch.'

Girl 6 thought she would make a point. She pretended to put a phone to her ear. 'Call me. Ring! Ring!! Go on . . .' The shoplifter felt uncomfortable and looked around to see if anyone was watching them. When he saw that no one was, the shoplifter picked up a pretend phone and called Girl 6 nervously. 'Ring! Ring!'

Girl 6 smiled at him teasingly – she wouldn't pick up. The shoplifter didn't hang up. 'Ring. Ring. Ring Goddamnit!'

Girl 6 mimed picking up a phone, paused, and used her sexiest voice. 'Hello? My name's Lovely, what's yours?'

The shoplifter thought a moment. 'Joe Schbotnick.'

Girl 6 couldn't have been happier to hear from Joe Schbotnick. 'Oooo, Joe, you have a really sexy voice. Where ya calling from?'

The shoplifter wasn't buying into this whole business, it was for losers, he'd make his point. 'I'm calling from death row.'

Girl 6 didn't miss a beat, 'Death row. Oooh. You must be a dangerous man.'

'That's right. Fucking A man.'

Girl 6 knew that the shoplifter thought he couldn't be hooked. She also knew that he was wrong. 'Can I tell you what I look like?'

The shoplifter was thinking about more pie – but he'd go along with Girl 6's game. 'Shoot. Fire away.'

Girl 6 paused and saw the shoplifter look at her with expectation. 'I've got dark hair. Big dark sensuous eyes. I'm five-foot six-inches and my best features are my big breasts. They're forty double D's.'

She had the shoplifter's attention. He was drawn into the fantasy and was an astonished man. 'Bitching forty double D's Dude,' the shoplifter blurted.

The shoplifter's pile of empty pie plates was stacked up on the table. The shoplifter was totally focused on Girl 6's performance. He was mesmerized. Girl 6 was also separated from reality. She was 'on' and completely lost in the act. There was an added dimension for Girl 6 during this particular exhibition. Normally her audience was unseen and anonymous – their reactions diluted by the telephone and miles of fiber-optic distance. At the diner, however, her audience was only inches away and the strength of the shoplifter's response fueled her own. Girl 6 was transported, carried away – enraptured – by the eroticism and intimacy of the encounter. Girl 6 was no longer Girl 6 sitting in a diner at night with some horny guy eating pumpkin pie. Girl 6 was Dorothy Dandridge – a different person – entirely and completely. It was as real to her as the air she breathed.

'And then you'd ram your nice fat cock down my sweet little throat. Oooh. I'm a deep throat, Joe.'

The shoplifter hadn't blinked his eyes in several minutes. Sweat was breaking out on his forehead. All he could do was mutter 'Goddamn' in quiet awe.

A fourth empty pie plate had joined the shoplifter's stack. Girl

131

6 had slipped out of Dorothy Dandridge and was now riffing as the Mod Sister. 'And I want your cock so bad Sweet Daddy. You like that Mr Joe Schbotnick?'

The shoplifter did. 'Fucking A man.'

A fifth plate of pie and Girl 6 was showing off her TV character, Esmerelda. The shoplifter wanted to hear more.

The sixth and seventh plates were done. The shoplifter had no idea he had eaten so much. He sat leaning back in his chair, mouth hanging open, tongue unconsciously licking his lips. The shoplifter's phone hand fell to his lap finding an iron-rod hard-on that was clearly depriving his brain of oxygen. He chewed a piece of pie slowly. His eyes never left Esmerelda's face.

'Come in my mouth, baby. I'm your little wet slut. Come all over me, Joe Schbotnick. Come all over my big horny tits.'

They left the diner and the shoplifter was now a convert. Until now, he had thought he had known Girl 6 intimately. 'Damn. I didn't know you were such a freak.'

Girl 6 enjoyed his surprise. 'Always have been. You never brought it out in me.'

The shoplifter spotted an alley and tugged on Girl 6's arm. 'I wanna show you something.'

'What?' There was nothing the shoplifter could offer that Girl 6 wanted to see.

The shoplifter put Girl 6's hand to his aroused crotch. Girl 6 wanted no part of that. She had just been making a point to the shoplifter. There had been nothing personal in her conversation. The shoplifter had taken it entirely too seriously.

'Hey! Are you crazy? Don't be putting my hand on your shit.'

The shoplifter didn't hear; he was in love. 'I've missed you, girl.'

Girl 6 got mad. He actually thought she owed him something. 'Leave me alone! Leave me the fuck alone! That's why I left your ass in the first place.'

The shoplifter was genuinely surprised. He couldn't believe

that Girl 6 had just been acting. In his mind, Girl 6's dialogue had started as a game and then become something else altogether. It had taken on a life of its own. 'Sorry. What did you expect? Talking to me like that.'

The shoplifter had crossed a boundary and Girl 6 was not happy. 'I was just playing.'

'I don't play like that.'

Girl 6 had had enough. She was done with him. 'You sick bastard. Go home to your mother and leave me alone.' Girl 6 glared at the shoplifter and then walked out of the alley.

The shoplifter knew he had fucked up. He hadn't meant to, but he couldn't help himself. It wasn't his fault. Girl 6 had done all the talking.

# CHAPTER TWENTY-TWO

The nights and days ran together. It was early morning and Girl 6 was in her cubicle with her head down on the desk, dozing. It was pointless to go home. She was too exhausted, her mind racing too fast to get a decent night's sleep before she would have to come back. She was beginning to have a difficult time distinguishing between memories from her real life and memories from her fantasy phone life. Had the shoplifter stood her up at Coney Island or was it someone else? Who else could it have been? Girl 6 ran through a mental Rolodex of names. It had to have been Bob Regular – he was the only one she cared about, the only one who could have hurt her. But why was the shoplifter on her mind? She had seen him recently. Was it recently? Or was it a memory from long ago when they had been together? Had she really been married to the shoplifter? Or had it been Bob Regular? Jimmy? Caller 30?

Girl 6's phone began to flash and her computer monitor beeped. Totally lost in her fatigue, she heard the noise but wove it into her frantic reverie along with the other fragments of reality. There was an alarm going off in her head, but she wasn't sure what it was warning her about.

In the lounge, Lil was throwing a party. All of the women working that shift were celebrating. Girl 29 blew a roll-out paper noisemaker at everyone and thought it was hilarious. Normally Lil would have been annoyed but today was different – a party had different rules from everyday life. Lil and Salesgirl 1 had gone all out. Streamers and balloons hung from the ceiling. Displayed on a cleared desk was an elaborately decorated cake and a large bowl of heavily spiked punch. The music was loud and some of the women danced together. Ronnie the security guard – who had been captivated at different times by Girl 15's sex talk – took a chance and grabbed her away from Girl 4. The others cheered as Ronnie led Girl 15 in an enthusiastic but awkward dance.

Girl 12 was a new hire. Tonight was her first night on the job and it had been a good one. Girl 12 had made her third caller come. She wore her corsage proudly and enjoyed being part of the celebration. The job was turning out to be different from what she had expected. Girl 12 wasn't exactly sure what the celebration was all about. She hadn't expected the group warmth and camaraderie. She had just walked into the room, and was too shy to ask what was going on. She noticed Lil's most recent motivational poster. Girl 6 had been leaving the competition behind. The poster declared, 'Most Minutes: Girl 6. Most Requests: Girl 6.' Girl 12 assumed the party was a celebration of Girl 6's accomplishments.

She was wrong, though, and one of the other women filled her in. Girl 19 was engaged and this was her send-off party. Lil was always happy when her girls got married. It was probably Lil's conservative upbringing; despite her own business success she still thought women were better off if they didn't have to work. Lil gave Girl 19 a maternal hug. 'Congratulations. We're going to miss you.'

Girl 4 noticed that someone was missing. 'Where's Miss 6?'

Girl 42 danced past her and shouted with a carnival barker's insistence, 'Working, working, working!!'

Lil let Girl 19 out of her arms and looked at her ring. 'It's lovely.'

'He went all out. Spared no expense.' Girl 19 couldn't have been prouder. There was no one she wanted to impress as much as Lil. Girl 19's fiancé had wanted to drop in for the party. He was so thrilled to be engaged that he had wanted to buy magazine subscriptions from each and every girl in her office. He didn't care what he bought – *Ladies Home Journal*, *Newsweek*, *GQ*, *Guns and Ammo*, *Popular Mechanics* – it didn't matter. He just wanted to spread the good cheer around. Girl 19 explained to him that company rules prohibited anybody other than employees from being on the premises, something about insurance regulations. She hated lying to her fiancé but figured it was only a white one. Lil would have been proud of how quickly she had come up with just the right response to keep her fiancé out of the office without hurting his feelings. Girl 19 wondered if she'd ever have a job again where success was gauged by how well you spun the bullshit. She didn't think about it too long, though. She didn't plan to ever work again if she could help it.

Girl 29 blew her noisemaker into Girl 19's ear. They hugged and then Girl 19 pushed her away before she could blow the toy again. Girl 29 had drunk her share of punch, ran across the room, and opened the door to the operators' work room. She stuck her head inside and blew her noisemaker as loudly as she could.

Girl 6 didn't hear her. She had woken up from her half-conscious state and was now the only woman working. Girl 6 was focused on her call. Her caller had a special fantasy and had asked her if he could tell her about it. That was fine with Girl 6.

Caller 33's fantasy went on for a long time. The party continued for hours. Girl 6 went to the bathroom to be by herself and clear her mind, but she couldn't escape Caller 33's conversation. It stayed in her mind and Girl 6 replayed it over and over again in her head even as she tried to refresh herself for the next caller.

'You're this hot co-ed bitch and I'm the principal of the school.'

'Oh, yeah.'

'And everyone's complaining 'cause you're too hot and turn everyone on too much.'

Girl 6 put on some lipstick as she remembered her response.

'I get 'em hard and that's distracting. Are you hard right now, Tommy?'

'Sure am. Now, I'm the principal and I have to discipline you.'

Girl 6 understood Caller 33's desires. 'Yes, Mr Principal.'

In the lounge, Girl 19's engagement party hadn't slowed down. Girl 39 was telling tall tales to her friends – a group of veteran story tellers if ever there was one – and had them laughing out loud. Some had tears in their eyes. Girl 39 was telling them the raucous details of a caller's fantasy with only a little exaggeration mixed in. The women were laughing not only at the ridiculous happenings involved but also at the humor inherent in what they did.

'He had the phone in one hand and his cock in the other. What he was steering the car with I dunno. He came really big. Big wads of stuff and then kerblammo! I read about it in the paper the next day. He'd gone off the road and into the sea. Highway 1. That's when I was in LA. That's the highway out there.'

If Girl 6 had been in the lounge she wouldn't have been receptive to the joke. She just wouldn't have gotten it – not any more. There was a reason she wasn't with her friends celebrating Girl 19's engagement. Girl 6 applied makeup to her face, trying to live up to the imagery she created every night. Caller 33's voice floated in her memory. She enjoyed the sound of it. She enjoyed what Caller 33 had to say. The satisfaction she provided to callers was in some surprising way returning back to her. She fed their hungers and pumped up their self-images. After all this time, their satisfaction was beginning to provide Girl 6 with a personal sense of success, desirability and glamor. It was a feeling she had only associated with movie stardom. They wanted her. Men across America wanted her. They would pay to talk to her. They would pay to masturbate to her beauty and performance. Girl 6 was popular. Girl 6 was desired.

Caller 33 had wanted Girl 6 to 'Unzip my pants and suck me off.'

Girl 6 had agreed. 'Okay. You just take my head and shove it down on your cock.'

Caller 33 thrilled in the power Girl 6 gave to him. 'Suck me off you little slut. You need to be trained.'

Caller 33 had phoned from his Wall Street office. He was a man in his forties, a man who, by any standards, had been successful in life. Caller 33 had gone the Ivy League route after prepping at Deerfield. Caller 33's father, uncles and both grandfathers had gone to Princeton and he did the same. After college he had joined the brokerage house where his father had been a partner for thirty years. Caller 33 was a nice guy but no genius. He was accepted at the firm in deference to his father. Caller 33 had a nice office, little power, and plenty of security.

After a few years on the job, Caller 33 married a girl from a prominent Philadelphia family. Their wedding had been profiled in the Sunday *New York Times* and his wife quit her job. Caller 33 and his family lived on the Upper East Side and had a summer house in the Hamptons. Jerry Della Famina would welcome him personally at his restaurant. Caller 33's name was listed on various charitable letterheads and his nights off were often spent at fundraising parties at the Met, the public library, the Museum of Natural History, Lincoln Center – wherever rich people went to spend time with people like themselves.

The only glitch in Caller 33's charmed life was his wife's lack of sexual imagination. Caller 33's wife came from an old money, conservative family. She had conservative values. She had conservative values about money. She had conservative values about moral issues. She had conservative values about art, conservative values about politics. Finally, and most annoyingly to Caller 33, she had conservative values about sex. While she was innocently affectionate and most often willing to go to bed, Caller 33's greatest disappointment in life was that his wife was usually passive – actually, inert.

Caller 33's wife was an advocate of the 'protestant work ethic.' She understood that her husband had needs but she also felt that he should just get on with it. She was willing to do her part as long as she didn't have to do too much. Often she would lie on her back and think of things to do the next day – shopping to be done, invitations to send, children's school careers to monitor –

138

while her husband went about his business. She was particularly pleased that her husband was efficient with his attentions and she was usually able to catch Leno's monologue before falling asleep.

Caller 33 had a strong imagination and felt terribly let down by his wife. He knew there was nothing he could say to her. He knew that she couldn't change and that she would be hurt if he asked. Magazines didn't do much for him because they were no less inert than his wife. Caller 33 had seen phone sex profiled one night on *Prime Time Live* and chuckled disapprovingly along with the other couples he was sitting with. It took Caller 33 a few months before he got the courage to call. But tormented by nearly obsessive thoughts of a new office worker who looked surprisingly experienced for a woman of her young age, Caller 33 had finally rung up Lil's service.

Now, after several months of talking with Girl 6, Caller 33 had found an outlet for his needs. He had been working late on a meaningless project and the office was empty. He figured he had earned the right to some diversion. Caller 33 leaned back in his leather chair as he listened to Girl 6.

'I'm such a little fuck slut. Please, Mr Principal, come in my hot mouth.'

Caller 33 had a request. An order actually. 'Bend over my desk.'

Girl 6 agreed. She always agreed. Not like most of the people Caller 33 worked with who often said 'no'. She was always willing to try new things.

Caller 33 had become quite fond of Girl 6 and wanted to tell her so. 'I'm gonna fuck you good.'

Girl 6 sounded thrilled to hear it. 'I'm so wet.'

Caller 33 was a happy man. This language would never have flown on Sixty-Third Street. 'Tell me how bad you need it, tell me.'

Girl 6 did as she was told. 'I need it so bad, man.'

Caller 33 wanted to hear more. It wasn't enough that she

needed it. He needed her to need it like it was life or death. 'That's good. Beg for it, bitch.'

Girl 6 knew he was getting off by exerting his power over her. She'd throw in a 'sir' or two. She knew he liked that. 'Give it to me hard, Sir.'

Girl 6 was right. Caller 33 loved hearing the word 'sir.' It kept things on a civilized, polite level. Caller 33 was about to come but still needed absolution from a nagging sense of guilt. 'You'd fuck anybody and anything.'

Girl 6 knew what he wanted. Caller 33 needed to know that anything that happened between them was actually her doing. She had seduced him into this behavior. 'Yeah. I'd fuck anything 'cause, yeah, I'm so bad.'

The memory of the conversation ended and Girl 6 stared in the mirror of the bathroom, saying nothing, doing nothing, thinking nothing.

Things had quieted down in the lounge and Girl 39 was telling more stories. 'That's nothing compared to the old door. It's got bullets in it. One of Mistress Tawny's slaves comes over here to service her in person. Ronnie wouldn't let him in so he shoots the door down.'

Girl 12 couldn't believe what she was hearing. Girl 39 knew that Girl 12 was buying every word.

'Then he breaks down crying. Lil gave me the door. I got it at home. Drew a heart around each hole. It's a collector's item.'

Girl 19 leaned into their conversation to share some of her own good news. 'Tomorrow's my last day.'

Girl 39 was pleased for Girl 19 and not at all jealous though she knew that's what Girl 19 wanted. Girl 39 didn't want some guy, now matter how nice, taking over her life. 'Lucky you. Damn! That's a rock.' Girl 39 was an expert at making people think they had achieved the response they wanted.

Girl 19 was pleased that Girl 39 was jealous. Now she could feel sympathy for her single friend and spoke in a voice meant to sound consoling. 'He went all out. Spared no expense.' The patronizing comfort of her voice said to Girl 39 that she could have a ring and a husband too, soon enough.

The party ended eventually and the women who were going to work plugged themselves in while the others went home. Lil looked around the operators' room and saw that Girl 6 wasn't at her desk but hadn't signed out either. Lately Lil had been a little worried about Girl 6 and headed for the bathroom. She wasn't surprised to find Girl 6 sitting motionless on the sink. Lil used her kindest, most motherly voice.

'You all right Honey?'

Girl 6 turned towards Lil slowly. Her face was entirely blank. Girl 6 was trained to keep people happy. 'Don't I look all right?' She knew that's what Lil wanted, but Lil wasn't buying it tonight. She had seen this before, although never quite as bad as this.

'You look like shit. All right. Down off that sink. I'm sending you home right now. Take a couple of days off, you're burnt out.'

Girl 6 wanted to keep Lil happy, but she also wanted to keep working. Girl 6 knew that she had to stay on the phone just as much as she needed to eat and breathe air. She had never denied Lil anything before. 'No, I'm chill.'

Lil wasn't taken in. 'It's okay. I know what I'm talking about.'

Girl 6 didn't believe it. 'I'm on leave?' How could she be on leave? She was the top girl. She was ahead in every category that counted.

Lil was firm. 'Yep, you're on leave. Take some time off. Recharge your batteries. You'll be as good as new.'

Girl 6 was furious. 'I need to make this money.'

Lil knew that Girl 6's belligerence was a symptom of the problem. 'I'm not changing my mind.'

Girl 6 flounced off the top of the sink and bolted from the bathroom. She stopped at a pay phone across the street from the phone-sex office. She pulled a scrap of paper from her purse and dialed a number. She had kept the number all these months. Maybe she'd always known that someday she would be making this call. A woman's voice answered. After a few pleasantries, Girl 6 got to the point of the call. 'Is that job still available?'

Down in Midtown at the Manhattan Follies, Boss 3 tossed her little dog an M&M. She smiled to herself. She had known that Girl 6 would call back. She took pride in her ability to read people. She was curious, though, why Girl 6 had changed her mind now. 'If I may inquire, why the change of heart?'

Girl 6 wanted the job but didn't want to waste a lot of time. 'I got my own phone.'

Boss 3 appreciated Girl 6's businesslike manner.

After talking with Boss 3, Girl 6 bought some flowers from a Korean grocery and took a cab to Mount Sinai Hospital. She had seen enough news reports to know where Angela King's room was. Girl 6 found the long-term convalescent care facility and looked for a room decorated with cards, stuffed animals, balloons and flowers. Girl 6 walked as though she knew where she was going and no one bothered to question her. Girl 6 found Angela's room and waited while a nurse finished attending to the little girl and left.

Girl 6 hesitated a few moments to make sure that no one else was around. When the coast was clear, Girl 6 slowly opened Angela's door and looked inside. Angela was lying in bed, unconscious with IV tubes in her arms and an oxygen mask over her face. Girl 6 could hear the rush of the oxygen being forced into the little girl's lungs. Girl 6 knew it was trite, but she was amazed at how peacefully Angela lay there. Girl 6 was moved as she hadn't ever been moved before. It was one thing to hear the stories, see the pictures – it was another thing altogether to be in the same room with the girl. Girl 6 felt a momentary panic. She wasn't sure what she was doing there. Was she trying to help the girl like the movie star did? Was Girl 6 hoping to find something in the little girl's reaction that would make her feel like the movie star? Was it a selfish act? Girl 6 looked at Angela and found some peace – she knew that, for some reason that she didn't yet understand, she was supposed to be there. That was enough. Explanations could wait. Girl 6 leaned forward and kissed Angela on the cheek.

'May I help you?' The nurse had returned and was walking into the room briskly. She was not pleased to see Girl 6. 'You'll have to leave right now.' The nurse took Girl 6's arm roughly and led her into the hallway. 'Are you family?'

Girl 6 tried to offer the right response quickly – something she did every night at work. 'Uhh huhhn.'

The nurse wanted to know her name. Girl 6 had a character ready. 'My name's Brown. Lovely Brown.' Girl 6 slipped into her Girl Next Door persona. She figured the nurse would prefer Lovely to the dominatrix Miss April.

The nurse consulted a list, repeating 6's name as her eyes read down the columns, 'Brown, Lovely.'

Girl 6 in her most earnest voice tried to explain further, 'I'm her dad's youngest sister.'

The nurse finished the list and hadn't found anything. 'Lovely Brown is not down here.' Her voice told Girl 6 that she would have to go.

Girl 6 tried again. 'Took the bus up from Virginia, been ridin' all night.'

This sounded credible. The nurse wasn't sure what to do. She explained the problem. 'We've had so many impostors.'

Girl 6 replied with cheerful indignity, 'Don't I look like family?'

Girl 6 had taken her routine just a little bit too far. The nurse saw through her act. She didn't understand what made Angela such a touchstone for all sorts of people. She didn't understand why Angela had a room full of toys, cards and flowers while half-a-dozen other kids on the floor had nothing. The nurse contained her anger and knew that was just how things were sometimes. She wanted this 'family member' off her floor but figured maybe Angela could get something beneficial out of her. 'Why

143

don't you leave the flowers with me? I'll make sure she gets them. Thanks for stopping by, dear. Oh, and if you'd like to help the family out with the bills, make your check out to the Angel Angela Fund and leave the check with me, okay?'

Girl 6 took a last look at Angela. She was embarrassed to be caught out in her lie and mumbled something to the nurse. Girl 6 wasn't used to a scrutinizing audience. Her callers wanted to believe and Girl 6 was momentarily shaken that her skills had failed her when she needed them. Girl 6 said something about not having a check and that she'd send one in the mail.

The nurse crossed her arms and sighed as she watched Girl 6 hurry out. What did these people want from this little girl? She just couldn't understand it.

# CHAPTER TWENTY-THREE

Girl 6 walked in from the street wearing sunglasses. In the dilapidated lobby of the old hotel, she opened her mailbox and pulled out junk mail. She was about to swear when she spotted a brown envelope shoved towards the back. Girl 6 reached in and pulled it out. After looking at the return address, Girl 6 ripped open the envelope, pulled out a cassette tape and a brown instruction book. Girl 6 smiled.

Girl 6 sat on her bed and read through the instruction book. Next to her on the bed was an old-fashioned, heavy, black dial phone. Girl 6 had bought it at a thrift shop on Broadway. It wasn't pretty but it would do what she needed it to do. She popped the cassette into her tape recorder and hit play. Boss 3's voice began to speak to her.

'If you do decide to accept this mission you must realize your own private line is essential. I suggest getting your number unlisted and inaccessible to caller ID. Choose a phone with a lightweight receiver. I suggest a headset. That way your hands are kept free.'

Girl 6 hadn't thought of that. All she could say was, 'Huh.' She should have known.

Girl 6 was twenty minutes into the tape and hadn't moved an inch from her bed. Her attention was focused upon Boss 3's instructions. 'While most office-bound fantasy girls are restricted to what they can talk about, a fantasy girl who works out of her home, a 'home girl,' experiences complete and total freedom. You can invite your caller to fully experience his deepest, darkest, wildest, strangest desires! No inhibitions! No restrictions! Total freedom! No taboos!'

Girl 6 knew this meant she'd be making more money than she'd made working for Lil. Money, however, was less and less important to her. She wanted new experiences. Girl 6 wanted a no-restrictions environment. She'd started to grow bored at Lil's once she learned that there was a basic routine to the calls. Girl 6 had grown numb to the shock she had initially felt at some of the more creative and exotic conversations. She knew that if she wanted the excitement to continue, she'd have to try new things. Girl 6 now wanted to – needed to – take the whole deal further. She was interested in some real adventure. Girl 6 was fascinated by the idea of how far guys liked to go. And Girl 6 felt compelled to discover how far she was willing to go herself. Girl 6 listened to the tape and studied the book.

Boss 3 brought her into the system quickly and Girl 6 was working regularly for her before many days had passed. Girl 6 sat on her bed and spoke with Caller 10. 'We'd be in the hallway and you'd be moving ya pink tongue in and out of my hot little pussy.'

Caller 10 interrupted her. 'We'd be in the hall. It would be really dirty and I'd be all over you.'

Girl 6 continued. 'You'd be sucking my tits, man. And then you'd turn me over and force ya cock up my ass.'

Someone knocked on Girl 6's door and she got up to answer it. Girl 6 looked through the spy hole and saw the shoplifter wearing a goofy leisure suit and holding some flowers he had swiped earlier in the day. Caller 10 didn't hear the knocking. 'I'm completely rock hard baby. I wanna come right up ya ass.'

The shoplifter saw Girl 6 eyeballing him through the door. He was surprised when she didn't say anything but just opened the door. He hadn't meant to bother her. Girl 6 stared right into the shoplifter's eyes as she sexed Caller 10. 'Oh, shoot it in me, big boy. Come all up my ass, come all in my mouth, come all on my lusty tits.'

The shoplifter's mouth went dry. He had prepared for a number of different scenarios – Girl 6 mad, Girl 6 surprised, Girl 6 this, Girl 6 that – but the shoplifter hadn't expected her to be sexing at home. He couldn't get a word out of his throat. Girl 6 shut the door in his face.

The shoplifter came back later that night. The change in Girl 6 was immediately apparent to him. Girl 6 was wearing a leather mini skirt and leather jacket. It was still Girl 6, but her wardrobe transformation reflected her change in attitude. She looked self-consciously hipper, as though she were living a faster lifestyle. The shoplifter was both aroused and disappointed by the difference. Still, she'd taken his flowers and was actually going out with him. That was progress. The shoplifter decided to approve, but changed his mind when Girl 6 talked about why she changed sex services.

'I quit the office. They're so tame. Tame and lame. I got something better going at home. Home cooking, you know? The pay's really great. I cook all night, you know?' Girl 6 was truly excited by the work she'd gotten from Boss 3's company. After the de-sensitizing repetition of Lil's office, Girl 6 found the new service tremendously exciting. Guys talked about anything and asked her to do things she didn't know could be done. She was exploring uncharted territory and was fascinated by the journey. The rule at Lil's may have been not to feel anything during the calls but with Boss 3's clients, Girl 6 was definitely feeling a lot. The money was better and she got off on the talk – Girl 6 didn't know why she had waited so long to leave Lil.

Girl 6 and the shoplifter ended up at The Wiz, an electronics superstore. Girl 6 and the shoplifter played with different things – walkie-talkies, computer video games, large-screen TVs, whatever they happened to come across. Girl 6 was actually having something closer to a date than she'd had in a long time. If she thought about it, Girl 6 wouldn't have been able to remember the last real date she had been on. Girl 6 and the shoplifter fooled around in an easygoing way. They were comfortable with each other. For the first time in months, Girl 6 wasn't performing in front of a man; she was simply being herself. The shoplifter's hopes rose a little. This was how he remembered her, warm,

147

funny, smart and playful. Maybe the Girl 6 he had once married was coming back to him. Maybe they would have a chance together again.

Girl 6 couldn't help but notice the latest news report on Angela King – it was playing simultaneously on a few dozen television sets. Her playfulness subsided and she seemed to go to a different and darker place. The shoplifter noticed the abrupt change and watched Girl 6 watching the news broadcast. He didn't understand what the big deal was. He knew she felt bad about the little girl, who didn't? But Girl 6's near obsession with the kid was strange. He just didn't get it.

When the news report finished, Girl 6's mood was clearly different. She took a cassette out of her jacket pocket and stuck it into one of the store machines. She hit play. The shoplifter didn't know what to expect. He was truly surprised to hear a recording of Girl 6's voice during a call.

'I'm a Black girl. That's what you wanted, right?'

Caller 35 had a request. 'Talk spicy.'

'Spicy?'

'Honey chile. You know.'

'Honey chile?'

Caller 35 knew just what he wanted. 'Honey chile, yo mamma. You know.'

Girl 6 understood. She spoke 'spicy': 'Yeah, sugar, I know.'

The shoplifter stared at Girl 6 with a 'you've got to be kidding' look. Girl 6 shrugged her shoulders – it wasn't her fantasy. 'I just do what they want.'

The shoplifter and Girl 6 strolled through different departments in the store. The shoplifter put on a pair of headphones, got distracted, and walked towards the telephone section. A salesclerk noticed the shoplifter walking off, caught up with him, and asked for the headphones back. The shoplifter and Girl 6 laughed. He had honestly forgotten that he was wearing them. For a moment, the shoplifter assumed the identity of a befuddled, normal shopper – not someone who made his living by stealing from stores like this one. He liked the presumption of innocence he got from the salesclerk who had seen dozens of distracted customers walk off while still wearing forgotten headsets. The shoplifter laughed, imagining himself to be a society register WASP aristocrat explaining to the pesky help. 'Ooops, sorry, stupid me, how dreadfully negligent.' The salesclerk laughed too and apologized for disturbing him. The shoplifter felt downright upright. Girl 6 just shook her head in amazement.

They moved on to the telephone department. Girl 6's eyes roamed lovingly over the amazing assortment of phones. The shoplifter thought she looked like a kid in a candy shop. Girl 6 went from phone to phone and started testing each one out. The shoplifter wasn't that concerned with the displays but was momentarily interested in watching Girl 6. The Wiz offered almost every phone imaginable – plain touch-tone phones, old-style dial phones, touch-tone phones with the buttons on the receiver, phones with clear bases and neon lighting, designer phones with 'hip' color schemes, Louis XV style gilded Versailles phones, Mickey Mouse phones, multiple-line phones, phones with faxes, phones with answering machines, phones with clocks built in, phones with little televisions built in, cellular phones, even an ersatz red English telephone booth. The shoplifter's mind wandered away from Girl 6 as his attention was drawn back to the other merchandise in the store. There was a lot of good stuff available. He was going to take a look.

Girl 6 played with a voice-changing phone and then tried on a light-weight telephone headset. She tested it out and decided to buy it on the spot. A clerk rang her up, put her purchase into a bag and gave her a receipt. The clerk was a friendly high-school kid and Girl 6 gave him a nice smile. She was pleased to have found the headset and happy to have spent the day in such an ordinary manner. If her feelings towards the phone job were approaching an addictive stage, she also enjoyed a reprieve from its intensity. Shopping with the shoplifter, making a perfectly normal, everyday transaction, topped off with an

149

innocent exchange of smiles gave Girl 6 a refreshing dose of normality.

As Girl 6 and the shoplifter walked out of the store an alarm went off. Girl 6 assumed that the kid behind the counter hadn't removed the security strip from her package. She stopped and shrugged as if to point out his error in a cheerful way. The clerk assumed the same thing and began to apologize, but before Girl 6 could return to the counter and before the clerk could speak, the shoplifter grabbed Girl 6's hand, dragged her out of the store and down the street.

Girl 6 didn't understand what was going on. One moment she had been Miss Everyday Citizen buying something and now she was being chased. All she could say was, 'What the fuck?'

The shoplifter didn't have time to explain. 'Run. Just run.'

Girl 6 wanted to stop and tell the guards that she had a receipt to pay for her purchase as tapes began to fall from the shoplifter's pockets – not just one, or three, or five, but it seemed like the whole fucking store. Girl 6 thought that all of The Wiz's racks must be empty, stripped clean. She knew that her explanation – her innocence – was now irrelevant. Girl 6 ran, actually pulling ahead of the shoplifter who was trying hard to keep the last tapes in his pockets.

Girl 6 and the shoplifter pushed through crowds. People yelled angrily as they were shoved aside. Girl 6 couldn't believe that this was happening to her. She couldn't believe that she was running from security guards. She couldn't believe that the people who were watching her assumed that she was a thief. Girl 6's fury made her run faster, as though she were trying to run away from herself.

The shoplifter pulled Girl 6 on to a side street where a construction site hid them from their pursuers. As soon as they were off the avenue the shoplifter walked slowly and made sure Girl 6 did the same. They tried to assume the identity of normal people out for a walk, but both were breathing too heavily from the exertion and had to stop. The shoplifter pulled a stolen cellular phone from his inside jacket pocket. He examined it, flipped it open and then pretended to dial, 'Ring, ring! Ring, ring!'

Girl 6 couldn't believe what she was hearing. All she could do was mutter in disbelief, 'Jesus.'

The shoplifter was persistent. 'Ring, ring!' He thought he was hilarious.

Girl 6 began to find her breath. 'No answer. I'm not picking up.' Her anger slowly subsided. Disgust and disbelief began to kick in. She couldn't believe that she'd fallen for the shoplifter's shit all over again, even if she'd only been duped for half a day. Girl 6 walked backward away from him. 'Stay away from me, okay? It's not gonna work out? Don't ever call me. Ever.'

The shoplifter began to sputter his defense but Girl 6 cut him off.

'Let's review the facts: Number 1, you're a criminal. Number 2, you're a lost cause. Number 3, you're a loser. So goodbye. End of story.' Her rage surged again and Girl 6 yelled in the shoplifter's face, 'ASSHOLE!'

She turned and walked rapidly back towards the avenue. The shoplifter watched her go, furious. Who did she think she was? Where did she get off with all this superiority bullshit? She was no better than he was.

# CHAPTER TWENTY-FOUR

Girl 6 worked the phones from home and sexed Caller 36. She sat at her vanity table dressed as a darkly perverse representation of the Girl Next Door. While the simple white blouse that she wore fit the part, the blond wig with pony tails pushed the outfit into the realm of depravity. Girl 6 was a lurid vision of imitation innocence, a pederast's dream, an impotent man's power. She was virginity and seduction simultaneously – completely absolving her caller of responsibility.

Girl 6 worked now in a profoundly different atmosphere from Lil's. At the phone-sex office there had always been a protective separation between Girl 6 and her callers. While conversations at Lil's were sometimes erotic, sometimes childish, sometimes fun and playful, sometimes sordid and hurtful, Girl 6 had always been cocooned by the bright fluorescent lighting and, more importantly, by the women sitting near her. The cubicles and the working women provided a sense of safety and sisterly camaraderie. While sometimes they took calls they didn't like, the women at Lil's shared a sense of being in it together. If Girl 6 was put off by a caller, she could unplug and go into the lounge for a maternal talk with Lil. The office provided anonymity and distance.

Working from her apartment, however, brought the caller directly into Girl 6's home. The tone of the callers could be erotic but were now more often deeply strange and disturbingly bizarre. The men who called the new service enjoyed violating taboos and got off on dangerous and violent fantasies. Girl 6 was fascinated by the conversations and increasingly attracted to the dark underground areas of these men's minds. Girl 6 was being consumed by her work.

Caller 36 was feeling stern. 'Daddy's gonna spank you good and hard 'cause you want it bitch, 'cause you need it.'

'I'm such a bad little girl.'

'You're such a bad little bitch. Pull up your skirt.'

Girl 6 moaned with anticipation. 'Oh, Daddy.'

'Now pull down your white cotton panties.'

Girl 6 clenched her eyes shut and opened them. She had been working twelve straight hours and was exhausted. She chose not to stop. 'Oh, Daddy.'

Caller 36 was getting his money's worth and had specific instructions. 'Raise your little hot ass up real high and lemme spank you bitch. Hurry up. Hurry up. My wife is coming home. Make me come.'

Girl 6 slapped the vanity table with a leather strap – sound effects.

Caller 36 didn't say another word. Girl 6 could hear noises over the phone but knew they weren't actual words, just grunts, groans, and moans, followed by silence. Caller 36 hadn't hung up but he was busy doing something other than talking. It didn't matter to Girl 6 – the more minutes the better. Her exhausted mind began to wander. Girl 6 heard an explosion of canned laughter and she dissolved into Esmerelda her phone sex TV character – appearing somewhere in Black sitcom land.

*Girl 6 as Esmerelda had the phone to her ear. The shoplifter's voice could be heard in the role of Boy on the Phone. 'Baby, baby, baby, baby.'*

*Girl 6 tried to warn the shoplifter. 'My parents are home.'*

*Jimmy as Girl 6's father grabbed the phone from her and shouted into it. 'Gimme that phone! Now look here son! You're speaking to the man of the house. Now, you better go on and get another girl to wipe your feet with, not my daughter and don't ever call here again. This is MY HOUSE!' Jimmy as the father slammed down the phone. Canned applause approved of the performance.*

*Lil as Girl 6's mother nodded her head and looked at her husband proudly. Jimmy as father turned to Girl 6 and spoke firmly but with warmth.* 'Honey, your mother and I want you to have an active social life, but when some sicko calls the house you don't . . .'

*The phone rang again, interrupting the lecture. Jimmy picked it up.* 'No you can't speak to her. I'm warning you.' *Jimmy slammed down the phone. The canned applause was loud.*

*Lil as Girl 6's mother spoke consolingly.* 'Listen to your father, Baby.'

*Girl 6 was defensively bewildered – she couldn't figure out what her parents were so upset about. She was surely a wronged person.* 'How was I supposed to know he was a sicko? All he kept saying was, can I come over? Can I come in? How was I to know . . .'

*Girl 6 did an exaggerated double-take as she realized what Jimmy was talking about. Her eyes widened with chaste dismay as a lightbulb went off in her mind. Lil as mother pressed her lips together and shook her head as she clucked disapprovingly. Jimmy as father clenched his fists and narrowed his eyes with a protective anger. Girl 6 could only chirp a virtuous,* 'Oh.' *The canned laughter and applause roared wildly.*

*The phone rang again. Jimmy picked it up.* 'Son, you are trying my patience.'

'But why can't I speak to her?' *the shoplifter whined over the phone.*

*Jimmy made a face to Girl 6 that promised a satisfactory resolution to the problem caller.* 'Hold on a second, son, she'll be right here.' *Jimmy as father put the receiver down and hurried over to the living-room closet.*

*Girl 6 and Lil shrugged in total bewilderment – what was father up to?*

*Jimmy returned with a twelve-gauge shotgun and blasted the telephone into smithereens. The little voice of the shoplifter was heard one more time.* 'Awww. Ya got me.'

*The family hugged as though all the problems in the world had been solved. The audio engineer in Girl 6's mind pushed the dials for the canned laughter and applause up to painful decibel levels.*

Girl 6 was ripped back to reality by the return of Caller 36. 'You're a little slut, aren't ya? Aren't cha?'

Girl 6 didn't disagree. 'Oh, yeah. Oh, yeah, baby.'

It was late in the east but not so late in the west and Girl 6 began to field calls from lonely men on the other side of the country. After hours on the phone her blond pony-tailed wig was pushed back on her head and Girl 6 could see her natural hair in the vanity table mirror. As she received instructions from the phone service's switchboard operator, Girl 6 prepared and set one of her brunette wigs. The operator was giving Girl 6 the name of a new client.

'Wojowski, Wo-jow-ski. Gregory. Got it?'

Girl 6 wrote down the best approximation of the name that she could figure out and replied through her fatigue, 'Yeah.'

The switchboard provided some background. 'He's living in Pasadena, but you don't know that.'

'Okay.'

The operator was bothered by Girl 6's lack of enthusiasm. If this was how lively she was when she sexed guys on the phone, Girl 6 wouldn't be working for Boss 3 for very long. She sounded dead, or at least deadened – barely able to pay attention.

'You listening?'

Girl 6 was listening. 'Yeah.'

The operator continued and made a note to her boss that Girl 6's calls should be monitored. 'He wants a fifteen-year-old. His neighbor's kid. Skinny as a rail. He saw her undress for bed. Wants to relive the experience.'

Girl 6 was ready to work. 'Got it.'

Girl 6 wore her new headset as she moved restlessly around the room with her eyes squeezed tightly shut. She was tired and already hated this guy Wojowski in Pasafuckingdena. Girl 6 was willing to do almost anything to anybody – over the phone.

Doing kids though, that was something that still managed to trouble her – even if it was just all talk. Hadn't Boss 3 said doing it over the phone kept the real thing from happening? Girl 6 was doing a good thing. Almost a public service like the department of children's services. Still, Girl 6 wasn't happy to have to field Wojowski's call. Why couldn't someone else have gotten it? Girl 6 would have much preferred an outlandish leather S&M fantasy – something that was clearly imaginary. Girl 6 rubbed her temples and looked out the window at the passing nightlife. Girl 6 saw lonely men and lonely women, a couple, some children. People were going around doing ordinary things. At least Wojowski's call wouldn't be boring. Outside of her apartment, the hallway payphone began to ring. The switchboard operator was giving Girl 6 more background on Wojowski. 'The girl he wants is a Black girl, this kid. Heavy accent.'

Girl 6 heard the canned laughter and applause again as her Black sitcom girl Esmerelda did her broad double-take. Her eyes widened with chaste dismay as a light-bulb appeared in her mind.

The operator was annoyed. 'Hey, wake up. You there?'

'Yeah, shoot.'

'His number is area code 818 . . .'

Girl 6's attention faded as she wrote the number down. Some-one began banging loudly on her door. The operator couldn't miss it. What the hell was going on with Girl 6. 'Whassat, your house caving in?'

'It's nothing.' Girl 6 took the rest of the number and ignored the person on the other side of her apartment door. Girl 6 began to dial Pasadena. As she did, Girl 6 slipped into character and awaited the pleasures of Gregory Wojowksi.

The call lasted almost an hour. By the time Gregory Wojowski came and went, Girl 6 had earned some good money. Pleased by the success of the call, Girl 6 took off her headset and realized that someone was still knocking on the door. After what the teenage girl from Pasadena had just been through, Girl 6 wasn't

156

intimidated by anything. Nothing would surprise her. Nothing could frighten her. Girl 6 opened the door and an angry Jimmy walked in.

'Are you deaf? I've been banging on that door for an hour.'

Girl 6 should have known it would be him. 'I've been busy!'

Jimmy dispensed with formalities and pleasantries. 'That's what I'm talking about. Your ex, what did you do to him? He wants you back.'

'I don't go back, only forward.'

Jimmy didn't know exactly how to respond to that, so he just continued on. 'Now I know I owe you money and I don't have a job but damn you and that damn phone! We don't even talk anymore.'

Girl 6 was tired and didn't want to explain herself to Jimmy. He had no hold on her. What had he ever done for her? She had been a friend to him, not the other way around. Girl 6 didn't need him. She had friends. She had a life outside of her little apartment. Jimmy had always been the semi shut-in. Spending all his time looking at sports pages and trying to figure out the next angle. Girl 6 had made an effort to be friendly to him because she had always felt bad for him. She didn't need some guy, barely more than an acquaintance, giving her shit for what she did.

'Jimmy, that's the thing. I get paid to talk now, I can't be bull-shitting with you.'

For all of his fixes and grandiose plans, Jimmy had a grounding in reality. He might not have known where he was going, but he usually knew exactly where he was. He couldn't believe what he was hearing from this woman who had once been pretty down to earth. He couldn't believe that all their time together – especially the time spent with her fantasy characters – seemed to mean so little to her. Jimmy knew that this situation was fucked. He knew that this wasn't the real Girl 6 talking to him. He knew that she was sinking into the sewer through the telephone line.

'Me and you, you and me having a normal conversation, two friends just talking, is bullshitting?'

Before Girl 6 could reply, Jimmy went over to the vanity table. He pulled off a letter that had been taped over a picture of Dorothy Dandridge. Jimmy read it, shaking his head. What was it doing taped there? Couldn't she see it for what it was? Jimmy assumed his whitest voice.

'Dear Miss Lovely. I'm such a baby and it's hard for me to go to sleep at night, I'm hungry. Mommy, please squirt some of your warm breast milk into my bowl of frosted flakes. THEY'RE GREAT! Love, Tony the Tiger.'

Girl 6 stared back defiantly at Jimmy. She was thinking of something to say – some reply that would shut him up. Girl 6 couldn't do it. She heard the letter for what it was and as hard as she tried to be pissed off – Girl 6 had to laugh. Jimmy laughed too. He laughed at the ridiculousness of the note but he laughed harder with the release of his tension. If Girl 6 hadn't been able to see the absurdity of it he would have had to admit that she was entirely lost. While Jimmy was happy to see that wasn't the case, he still wasn't feeling all that good. He needed to prod Girl 6 back to normality.

'All jokes aside, I wouldn't be surprised if you come on some of these calls, don'tcha, Miss Lovely?'

What was this guy's problem? Why did she have to take shit from him? Girl 6 figured that even if she was fooling herself about some things in her life, Jimmy was definitely fooling himself about his relationship with her. 'You're wrong about that. I know what's real and what isn't. Do you?'

# CHAPTER TWENTY-FIVE

Girl 6 had spent a lot of the night walking around upper Manhattan. Something about the pedophile caller from Pasadena and her argument with Jimmy made her feel the need to get out of the house. Girl 6 figured that she could have dealt with one or the other just fine. But to have to field both irritating incidents in one day put her on edge. She needed air and the illusion of being around normal people. Girl 6 didn't look at store windows as she walked. She didn't look at cars. She didn't look at buildings. Girl 6 focused on people's faces. She recognized a few in her own neighborhood without really knowing who they were. They were just people she had seen before in passing. The recognition added some sense of familiarity and made her feel less alone. Once Girl 6 got several blocks away from her street, however, she found the crowds to be less comforting. Even though she knew the odds were long, Girl 6 looked for faces that she recognized. When she realized that wasn't going to happen, Girl 6 looked for faces that might acknowledge her in a friendly, respectful way. The New York stare – straight ahead at some unseen point in the near distance – began to chip away at Girl 6's confidence. There were all these people and not one of them would affirm that she was a decent member of the community – not the briefest of smiles, not even the faintest of warm looks. Girl 6 felt cold, depressed, and angry.

Girl 6 found her way back towards Lil's neighborhood. She looked up and saw the bright lights of the phone-sex office burning. She would drop in for a visit. There was never anything like a 'welcome home,' even if you hadn't gone far away. Girl 6 was doing okay financially and decided to bring some gifts along to reward her old friends for being kind to her and to show them that she was doing well.

Girl 6 dropped in at the Pearl of Bombay Magazine Emporium and ordered a few cartons of cigarettes from the shopkeeper. She was surprised by his deferential attitude. She had expected him to be thrilled to see her after an absence and was sure he would hit on her. Girl 6 was surprised when there were no invitations to take vacations together, or for marriage, or for simple quick fucking in the back room. The shopkeeper merely repeated what Girl 6 asked him for, quietly listing off the names of the different cigarette brands. Girl 6 noticed that his 'Thief Beware' sign – with the photograph of the shoplifter – was still posted above the counter. Girl 6's anger built but she had no excuse for venting – the shopkeeper was being too well behaved.

Girl 6 was about to leave when she spotted the reason for the shopkeeper's good behavior. Girl 6 saw the shopkeeper's wife walk out from the back of the store and join him behind the counter. Girl 6 decided that she was going to fuck with the shopkeeper as his wife smiled warily at her.

'Do you still want to take me fishing?'

The shopkeeper ignored her and continued sticking her cigarette cartons into a plastic bag. His wife looked at Girl 6 as though she were insane. Girl 6 was just starting.

'Oh! Now you gonna try and play me.'

The shopkeeper turned apologetically to his wife and explained, 'She's crazy.' The shopkeeper's wife had seen plenty of lunatic customers and nodded her agreement. She hated New York and never thought that the money they earned in their store was worth the separation from their family in Bombay.

Girl 6 watched the shopkeeper carefully – loving every second of his discomfort. She could tell he was terrified that she would continue, that Girl 6 would reveal more of their past conversations.

Girl 6 gave him what he feared. 'Oh! Now you don't want to get married anymore, like you don't know me anymore. That's cold.'

The shopkeeper's wife was less and less certain of what was

going on. She noticed that her husband was much more concerned about this crazy lady than he normally was about lunatics off the street. The shopkeeper's wife began to worry. 'Who is this lady?'

The shopkeeper just wanted Girl 6 out of the shop. He was furious with himself for ever talking to this whore. Whores were trouble and wives always discovered them. He was going to have to be especially nice to his wife for the next few weeks to get past this one. Or maybe he shouldn't be nice at all – he wasn't sure. He was sure, however, that Girl 6 needed to leave quickly. 'Who is she? What else? Here just take the cartons and get out of here. Crazy lady! I don't want your money.'

Girl 6 grabbed the cartons, winked at the shopkeeper so that his wife could see, and raced for the door. The shopkeeper's wife knew that her husband didn't give things away to anybody. Not even family. The shopkeeper's wife knew enough about her husband to figure out that there must be something going on between this woman and him. Why else would he be trying to get rid of her by giving away so many cigarettes? Girl 6 turned around before she ran out the door and was happy to see the shopkeeper's wife beginning to give him some serious hell.

Girl 6 was feeling good as she made her way back to Lil's, oblivious to the shoplifter following her. He had spotted her about half an hour ago and had stayed with her, hoping to find a good time to bump into her. He had thought of following Girl 6 into the Pearl of Bombay but decided against it, knowing that the shopkeeper would have screwed things up for him. The shoplifter was angry. Why did some people have so much and others so little? Why shouldn't he have money, food, things, and most importantly – the girl? It was a fucked-up world and if he didn't get what he wanted he had no choice but to resort to other methods. Take and you shall receive – you couldn't argue with that.

The shoplifter watched carefully and stealthily, but his face showed only his fatigue and sadness. He knew he had screwed up with her before, but he was still hoping that he could somehow make things right. He thought about stealing her something nice, but the shoplifter knew that wouldn't work with Girl 6 any more. He wasn't sure where she was going, and the shoplifter closed in. He experienced an unrealistic surge of optimism and convinced himself that this time he could really steal her heart. He knew humor wouldn't work on her, not this time. The shoplifter had to come up with something else. He just didn't know what. Girl 6 knew that she was incapable of correcting his ways. She had once hoped she could and he had once played her along. As the shoplifter fell in a few people behind Girl 6, he deluded himself into thinking that he could change – would change – for her. He was about to call out her name when he noticed that Girl 6 was approaching Lil's office. The shoplifter hung back as Girl 6 pressed a buzzer.

Inside Lil's office, Ronnie the security guard looked at his video monitor and saw Girl 6. Girl 6 looked directly into the security camera, smiled, and shouted, '6 for sex!' Ronnie was happy to see her and got up out of his chair to let her in. The monitor showed her entering the building and then caught the dejected face of the shoplifter as he stepped into frame. He looked into the camera angrily, then appeared lost, hurt and – finally – rejected. He shoved his hands deep into his pockets, chewed his lip, frowned, and walked away.

Ronnie led Girl 6 inside and watched as she was reunited with her old friends. Girl 6 had always bought snacks for Ronnie and made sure that she flirted just enough for him not to think he was a loser. Ronnie was pleased to see that Girl 6 was doing okay. She had left so abruptly. As far as he knew, she hadn't left for something better. She hadn't gotten engaged like Girl 19 and she hadn't gotten a part in a movie or play like she told him she wanted. Lil had said that Girl 6 needed some time off – that she'd been burnt out. Ronnie had been around long enough to know that needing some time never meant anything good. Seeing her now, Ronnie figured that, whatever Girl 6 had been through, she was now over it. That was good news.

Lil looked up and saw Girl 6's return. She wasn't as happy as Ronnie because Girl 6 had already called her about the new job. Lil didn't approve of girls working from home. She knew the type of calls they got. She had hoped that, once Girl 6 experienced a few of the new callers, she wouldn't put up with it and would come back where she belonged. Seeing her now, though, Lil could tell that Girl 6 was on some sort of victory lap and that she wasn't looking to come back. Lil would go out and say hello a little later. There was no reason to rush. There was no reason to celebrate. Lil knew what those kinds of calls did to women.

Girl 6 was thrilled to see her old friends. She hadn't entirely realized how isolating working at home was until she stepped into the lounge. Girl 39 told Girl 6 how much she missed her. She didn't have anybody to really talk to at Lil's anymore. Everybody told Girl 6 how good she looked, which wasn't strictly true. Girl 6 looked like she spent her life indoors and didn't get enough sleep. Girl 6 worked hard to let them know she was doing just fine. She told them about how her income had shot up with the new job and they were all impressed. All of them wanted to know about the callers. They wanted to know about her conversations with them. What did they talk about? What did they like to do to her? Girl 6 took a perverse pride in describing the nature of the home calls. She could see the shock in some of her friend's faces when she told them a diluted sample of her callers' requests. Girl 6 showed off some more and told them about Gregory from Pasadena and the fifteen-year-old he fucked. The talk stopped and the moment became uncomfortable. Girl 6 realized she'd said too much, gone too far telling them about her exploits. She could see what they thought of what she was doing. Girl 6 changed the subject and soon everyone was enjoying themselves as they caught up on less dangerous subject matters. Girl 6 didn't really care what they talked about – recipes, the soaps, or brutalized sex – it was all the same to her. She was enjoying being out of the house. When the phones rang in the operators' room, however, Girl 6 felt uncomfortable. She felt she should answer. She knew there was a caller on the line. There was money to be made. There were fantasies to fulfill. Girl 6 had a sudden need to go back to her apartment and plug herself in.

# CHAPTER TWENTY-SIX

It was summer and New York began to close in on Girl 6. The smells of spoilage and the groping humidity were inescapable. Girl 6 dealt with matters practically by moving to a better apartment in the same building, buying a powerful fan, and spending her days in only her bra and panties. The windows to the street were wide open, and if she ignored the stench of urine and rotting garbage Girl 6 could convince herself that the climate was tropical and the winds sultry. Girl 6 as Dorothy Dandridge as Carmen Jones awaited her Harry Belafonte.

Girl 6's new home was a real apartment. It had a small but separate kitchen and a view of Queens to the east. Girl 6 also had a bedroom now but rarely seemed to use it. She'd work until she couldn't work any more and then collapse on the couch by an open window. Girl 6 put a pot of water on the stove and started her day by playing her messages. As the tape rewound, Girl 6 went into the bathroom to gargle. Later she'd do vocal exercises to keep her voice in shape for the day's performances. Boss 3 was the first caller and she spoke in her irritatingly demanding manner.

'Hey, honey, it's me calling from command central – can you take three of Niki's regs today? She's got the flu, call ASAP. Wake up and call me back. *Ciao.*'

The machine beeped and posted the time and date. Jimmy was next.

'It's Jimmy, you never call back. I never see you. What's going on?'

Girl 6 sat on the toilet and brushed her teeth as the machine beeped again. Boss 3 was getting impatient. 'It's me again. ASAP. Wake up! Call me. *Ciao.*'

Girl 6 slipped off what she was wearing and stepped into

the shower. Girl 39, from Lil's, called next and was annoyed. 'What's with ya? Weren't we going to have lunch? I've been here – an hour plus. All you do is stand me up these days, Lovely-dovely. Uncool, Kid. Mistress Tawny ain't interested in yer bull-shit, baby.'

Girl 6 heard Girl 39 and remembered that they were supposed to have lunch downtown that day. She had missed it. She didn't care. She had left Girl 39 waiting for over an hour. She didn't care. Girl 6 had worked the phones all night and had been to some pretty unusual places. She would shower, have something to eat and get ready for more calls. That was what mattered to Girl 6. The calls were what interested her. Why go out with Girl 39 and talk about the same bullshit? Girl 39 had nothing new to say, nothing really interesting, certainly nothing fascinating. But the callers did. Girl 6 wanted to go with them on their journeys. The callers put ideas into her head that she had never had before. The callers aroused her with fantasies she had never approached before. She was their fuck goddess and they would do anything for her. The callers worshipped Girl 6 and she was addicted to their adoration. No one, no one she had ever known, no person off the street, had ever given her this kind of satisfaction before. She didn't make them come – they came because of who she was. All across America, Girl 6 had men who venerated her – men who loved her, almost worshipped her. When Girl 6 was working she became something to her callers that was beyond Dorothy Dandridge, past Sophia Loren, and left Brigitte Bardot looking like a simple wannabe starlet. Girl 6 wasn't just a picture on a screen but an accessible goddess who charged by the minute. In the callers' grunts and groans, Girl 6 heard their prayers – and, like a beneficent deity, she usually answered them. Their needs gave Girl 6 tremendous power over them. Except Girl 6 needed them to call. She was nothing if they didn't call.

Girl 6 stayed in the steaming water while the answering ma-chine continued to play and beep insistently, a reminder that an outside world existed. The shower was a cleansing ritual for Girl

6. Anything she felt guilty about – and there was actually very little she did feel guilty about – was purified in the water. She made the water hotter, until it almost burned. Girl 6 stood directly beneath the shower faucet. The water massaged her forehead and her face. It cascaded down Girl 6's body, stinging but also soothing. She relished the pounding silence – no phones, no answering machines, no switchboard operators offering information on the next client, no husky voices approaching climax, no children being tied down and raped. In the safety of the shower, Girl 6 didn't have to hear their voices.

Girl 6 felt refreshed and rejuvenated. But the shower gave her more than silence. It also washed away her fear that she wasn't the person she wanted to be. If Girl 6 worried about having abandoned her acting career and her friends, the water offered warm and comforting absolution. In the shower there were no costumes, no roles to play. She was just herself – naked and free of pretense.

It was two in the morning and the sounds of traffic were lighter. The windows in Girl 6's apartment were wide open. The faded curtains blew inside as the winds brought in a thunderstorm from the Atlantic. Girl 6 sat at her vanity table dressed as Dorothy Dandridge as Carmen Jones and wore her headset. Girl 6 was sexing Caller 36 and was performing brilliantly. She was lost in her character.

'I just took a piss all over you and I want you to wear it for aftershave.'

'Yes, Mistress April.'

'You haven't been fucked in so long that you'll do anything for it, won't you?'

'Yes, Mistress April.'

'Bend over and take it up the old kazoo.'

Caller 36 appeared to be submissive but in reality he wasn't. He was paying for Girl 6's time and he decided he wanted to change things around a little. 'Yes, Mistress April, but I want us to switch now. You're my sex slave now.'

Girl 6 did as she was told. 'I'm hot and ready.'

Caller 36 walked the hallway of his apartment building slowly. A man hurried past him, but in the murk and squalor of the corridor he couldn't have seen much of Caller 36. The building was equally nondescript. It could have been anywhere – the Bronx, Baltimore, Portland, Cleveland, Sacramento. Caller 36 stayed in the darkness as he spoke with Girl 6. 'I've got the "Big A," bitch. What do you think of that? One foot in the grave. HIV positive.'

Girl 6 had dealt with guys who told her this before. 'Lemme suit you up.' The detail added credibility to the fantasy. Girl 6 could have almost laughed – most guys wished they didn't have to wear condoms – this prick fantasized about wearing one. However, this time Girl 6 was wrong. Caller 36 wasn't concerned with protecting his fantasy girl.

'Bareback, bitch. Up your ass. I got it from a slut. I'm gonna give it to a slut.'

Girl 6 froze. She had never been at a loss for words before. Caller 36 had just taken her into new territory. She had just experienced a new depth of baseness. Girl 6 was shaken. Caller 36 wanted to hurt her. He didn't just get off on hurting her; he wanted to get off by killing her. She had never participated in such a malevolent fantasy. Girl 6 started to wonder what sort of person would think up something like this. What pleasure could a person find in this shit?

The caller grew impatient. 'Hello?'

Girl 6 offered a stunned 'Hello?' in reply, as if she hadn't heard Caller 36 correctly.

Caller 36 was insistent and spoke harshly. 'I said up your ass. And beg me for it.'

Girl 6 went along. That was what she did. That was who she was. She did what the men on the other end of the phone demanded. Girl 6's voice lost its life. It was flat, deadened. 'Oh. Please gimme your cock.'

She hadn't done all that Caller 36 wanted. He reminded her. 'Up your ass.'

Caller 36 jerked himself off with one hand in his pants and covered his face with the other. With the hand over his face it was impossible to tell whether he was experiencing ecstasy or grief, or just hiding the authorship of his insane fiction from anybody who passed by him in the hall. He heard Girl 6 tell him what he wanted to hear.

'Up my ass.'

'Good and hard.'

'Good and hard.' Girl 6's voice sounded diminished over the cheap phone – as though it were disappearing into nothingness.

Girl 6 worked through the night. The storm off the ocean had passed though the city after a brief thunderstorm. Girl 6 lay on her bed in her blond pig-tailed wig with her Dandridge dress hiked up revealing her stomach. Girl 6 let the cooler, less fetid air wash over her skin. The clean feeling helped her project the virtuous nature of Lovely Brown. Caller 38 was astonished by something she had told him.

'You are kidding!'

Lovely was not kidding. 'Lucius. Lucius Thomas. That was his name.'

Caller 38 didn't have much of a sense of humor. 'Maybe it was Thomas Lucius.'

Lovely added more detail. 'He had thick glasses like the bottoms of Coke bottles.'

'And you kissed him?' Caller 38 couldn't imagine Lovely with such a loser.

Lovely's story was pretty tame. Girl 6 couldn't remember if it came from her own past or not. 'He kissed me first. I kissed him back. We were in kindergarten. We were in love. It was during a milk and cookie break.'

'Was he a good kisser?'

'I taught him a few things.'

Caller 38 had to laugh out loud. He knew Lovely Brown wasn't as pure as she made herself out to be. Caller 38 knew Lovely Brown to be pretty wild and willing to do anything for the boy she loved. 'Yeah. I bet you taught him a few things.'

'I wonder where Luscious Lucius Thomas is now?' Girl 6 asked aloud.

# CHAPTER TWENTY-SEVEN

Jimmy and the shoplifter shared a booth at the same diner where Girl 6 had sexed the shoplifter. The shoplifter felt lonely and looked sadly towards the booth where he had sat with Girl 6. Jimmy finished up a deluxe cheeseburger. The shoplifter helped himself to some of Jimmy's fries. Jimmy was trying to get the shoplifter through a tough period.

'Don't take it personally. She doesn't speak to me neither.'

The shoplifter didn't feel any better. If Girl 6 were talking to Jimmy at least she would have contact with the outside world. It was bad enough that Girl 6 wanted no part of him – it didn't help that he was worried about her as well.

'Guess she's working.' The shoplifter didn't like to think about Girl 6 taking shit over the phone. The shoplifter would have liked to climb through the phone lines and kick the crap out of the losers on the other end.

Jimmy watched the shoplifter's dejection grow. He tried to be helpful. 'I hear her sometimes through the door but I haven't seen her in weeks. Her phone's unlisted too. I'll give it to ya, but she screens all calls and she don't call back.'

Jimmy and the shoplifter's moods were sliding downhill fast. It bothered both of them to think of their Girl 6 locked in her room, sexing guys, and not spending any time with real people. They didn't know exactly what kind of calls Girl 6 was answering from home, but they knew there was something fucked with the whole setup. Both men had tried to get through to her in their own ways. Both men had failed. The shoplifter was nosediving.

'I miss her, you know? So if she could – I dunno. Meet me somewhere or something. I dunno.' The shoplifter didn't know what to do. Whatever problems he had gone through in life, he had always seen a way out. In most of those cases he hadn't really cared much one way or the other. Girl 6 was a whole different thing. He saw that now and wished he had seen it earlier.

Jimmy pulled out his wallet to pay his bill and tried to make the shoplifter feel a little better. 'I'll leave her another message.'

Later that night Girl 6 sat at her vanity table. For once, she wasn't working. Instead, she carefully wrapped a white bandage around her head. She looked at it and then looked at the newspaper photograph of Angela in the hospital. Girl 6 hadn't gotten the dressing exactly right. She unraveled it and then put it back on again – replicating the angle and position of the bandage on the injured girl's head. Girl 6 was entirely focused and transported. It took a while before she heard someone knocking on her apartment door. Girl 6 wasn't interested. 'We don't want none.' The pounding on her door continued, but Girl 6 didn't get up to answer it. Her hands went to her head and her face became contorted with pain. But her suffering wasn't caused by the noise from Jimmy's knocking. The pain was Angela King's, and now it was Girl 6's too.

Out in the hallway Jimmy's disgust and frustration were growing. It was bad enough that Girl 6 was wasting her money on an expensive apartment. He was more worried about the fact that Girl 6 didn't answer anyone's phone calls anymore. He couldn't believe that she wouldn't even open the door for him. Jimmy shouted, hoping to lure Girl 6 back to reality. 'What's with the new apartment? What happened to the money for LA?'

Girl 6 wanted nothing to do with losers like Jimmy. Guys like Jimmy were all about some always distant future. Girl 6 had a present, a job that made good money, a job she was good at, and the future wasn't her concern. She stayed at her mirror and shouted out to the hallway, 'LA ain't going nowhere but into the Pacific Ocean.' Girl 6 returned her attention to bandaging her head. She didn't notice the message on a white sheet of paper that was pushed underneath her door.

The night was almost finished, but there was still no hint of dawn in the east. Girl 6 lay on her bed, letting the cool air blow-

172

ing in from the street chill her, and felt more awake. She had picked up a call and was quickly flipping through her box of index cards trying to figure out who this caller was. Caller 30 couldn't believe that Girl 6 didn't recognize his voice. 'You don't remember me?'

Girl 6 was off to a bad start with Caller 30. She knew that recognition was a reason some of her guys called. In a solitary life, her callers felt special when Girl 6 knew who they were. It couldn't be helped. Girl 6 knew she had talked to Caller 30 before but didn't remember him.

'What're you into? That'll remind me.'

Caller 30 didn't respond right away. Girl 6 heard his labored breathing. Finally, he told her what he liked. 'I like it rough. Snuff. Remember me, wet bitch? Mr Snuffy? Mr Snuffy has connections. Mr Snuffy tracked you down.'

Girl 6 pushed her headset from her ear. Now she remembered Caller 30 and his fantasy of suffocating her in the green trash bag. Girl 6 wasn't sure what to do. She was almost done for the night and didn't want to deal with this asshole. Caller 30 didn't like waiting. He knew she had remembered who he was and rasped at her, 'Hello!?' Girl 6 tried to think it through but she was too tired. It was easier to talk with him than make a decision. What the fuck. It was only talk. She wasn't a nun – this is what she did. Caller 30 may be sick but his money wasn't. Girl 6 decided to take the call. Maybe she'd hear something she hadn't heard before. Maybe she'd like it a little. Girl 6 swung her headset down ready to go to work. All she heard was dial tone. Girl 6 wanted to make sure. 'Hello?! Hello?' Caller 30 was gone.

Girl 6 took a moment, knowing she'd played the call badly. Then she called the sex service switchboard to find out what had happened. 'Hey there. It's Lovely. Who'd you just send me?'

The operator didn't know what she was talking about. 'We didn't. Musta been a wild card.'

'Guess so.' Girl 6 didn't like it. Who had her number? It was unlisted. She had given it to only a few people. How had some crazy fucker gotten her home number?

Girl 6 hung up and lay on her bed without moving. Sleep overwhelmed her almost immediately. She wasn't even aware of its approach.

She was in Angela King's apartment building. In the hallway. Waiting at the elevator. No one else was around. There were no sounds from apartments. No smells from pots cooking on stoves. There were no signs of life other than Girl 6's consciousness. The elevator doors opened. She crossed the threshold apprehensively – driven by a compulsion she didn't understand. Girl 6 hung there for a brief moment caught between standing on her own – and the fall. She looked down and saw there was no elevator waiting for her. There was nothing to keep her from dropping – no safety net. Girl 6 plunged down the shaft and into the malignant void.

# CHAPTER TWENTY-EIGHT

Girl 6 stopped in for another visit at Lil's. When she walked in most everybody was hard at work. Girl 39, however, was taking a break and Girl 6 found her watching an old movie on TV. Girl 39 was pleased to see Girl 6 looking all right, but she was also wary. Girl 39 wasn't the type to either lecture a person or to worry about someone who didn't want to be worried about. She figured she could make her point without being too direct.

'You on tonight?'

Girl 6 thought she'd probably have a busy night although she wouldn't start until about eleven. 'Yep. Just came by to say hey.'

Girl 39 thought that Girl 6 was screwing up her life. 'Ya working too damn much.'

Girl 6 didn't agree and didn't disagree. She said, 'Maybe' and folded nine twenty-dollar bills into a piece of paper. She inserted the paper into an envelope. Girl 39 watched as Girl 6 addressed the envelope to Little Angela King, Mount Sinai Hospital.

Girl 39 was impressed that Girl 6 could afford to be so charitable. She didn't think, however, that the extra money was worth the price she figured Girl 6 was paying. Most people sent cards, dolls, flowers – but Girl 6 was sending almost two hundred dollars. Did she care that much about a little girl she had never met? Was she making payments against some debt of guilt? Girl 39 cared about Girl 6 but didn't know her well enough to understand the real reason why she was sending so much money.

Girl 6 licked the envelope shut. She was done. Girl 6 heard the phones ringing in the other room and got restless. Girl 39 could gauge her reaction and tried to get Girl 6 to stick around for a while. Maybe if Girl 6 spent some time in her old work environment and got to remember what it was like, all the women together, she'd choose to stop working at home.

'Sit for a bit,' said Girl 39. 'Miss an hour. Have a coffee.'

Girl 6 agreed but not enthusiastically. Girl 39 saw that Girl 6 was talked out. She had put so much of herself into working the phones that there was nothing left of the smart, funny kid who had come to work at Lil's six, seven, eight – however many months ago. Girl 39 tried to prime the pump.

'I bet you work around the clock.'

'Bingo.'

The conversation died. Neither had anything else to say to the other. There was a warmth of feeling but an inability to express anything any more. Words were money and they weren't to be wasted on casual talk among friends. Girl 6 was empty.

Lil walked in and noticed Girl 6 sitting silently with Girl 39. Lil was showing a new hire, Girl 18, around the office. Girl 6 looked at Girl 18 and saw that she was young, fresh and unjaded. Girl 6 stared at Girl 18 as she walked around the room taking a look at things. Girl 6 had a moment of self-recognition. Had she really looked like this kid – this child – when she had started working here? No, Girl 6 had never been this pristine. Was it possible that she had ever looked this naïve? Had she ever not known the hidden thoughts of anonymous men?

The nether world of the callers had usurped her own. There was little of her old life left nowadays. Girl 6 hadn't been to an acting class since the day Diane told her she couldn't carry her any more. Girl 6 had not seen a single one of those friends even though they had called. Girl 6 had left a message for her parents that she had been called suddenly to understudy a featured role in the touring company of *Beauty and the Beast*. She would be on the road for months and unavailable. She knew that by now they would have figured out her lie because she would have sent postcards from across the country if it had been true. Her parents knew she wanted to be left alone and were trying to figure out how to help her. None of it mattered though. Girl 6 was isolated from her life and now existed almost exclusively in the sweaty fantasy world of her callers. She hadn't planned for things to go this way, but that's how they had evolved.

Girl 6 watched Lil run down the rules with Girl 18. Her mood crashed as she realized that she had been exactly like this new girl. Girl 6 wanted to cry at her loss. What had happened to that girl? Where had she gone? Could she ever come back? Did Girl 6 even want her to come back? Girl 6 didn't know the answer but felt breathless with an intimate sense of tragedy and loss.

Girl 39 watched Girl 6 as she listened to Lil. 'This is the lounge. Coffee machine. We take up a donation once a month. TV, watch it with the headphones. Monitor on so you know when yer up. Oh, keep a notebook. A log. You'll remember your callers. They like that.'

Lil looked at Girl 6 and could see exactly what she was going through. Lil offered her a lifeline. 'I'm hiring if yer interested.'

But Girl 6 had gone too far to come back. She couldn't, not any more.

Lil didn't have the time or the interest to force the issue. 'Suit yerself. Coffee?'

Girl 6 started to say that she already had some but realized that Lil was asking Girl 18 – she had already moved on.

Girl 18 appreciated Lil's generosity. She turned to Girl 6 and introduced herself, 'Eighteen. Darleen.'

Girl 6 introduced herself. 'Lovely.'

Girl 6 started to put the cash-filled envelope into a pocket. Girl 39 stopped her. She wasn't sure she should. Girl 39 didn't know how Girl 6 would react. Maybe her caring for little Angela King was her last attachment to real, living people. Girl 39 didn't believe in sugar-coating facts. She made her money spinning fantasies but didn't think friends let other friends live in illusion.

'They released her today.'

Girl 6 wasn't sure who she was talking about. Girl 39 pointed to her envelope. Girl 6 was surprised. 'Yeah?'

'Yeah. Released today. She walked out on her own. Sorta.'

Girl 18 knew they could only be talking about one person, one news story. 'She made the six o'clock news.'

Girl 6 was happily stunned. 'Wow!'

Lil didn't like what she was seeing. 'Where ya been, 6? In a coma? Darleen, let's get you on your first call.'

Lil bent over and whispered into Girl 39's ear. 'Get a flower ready, okay?' Lil started out of the room to lead Girl 18 to the phones. Girl 18 stayed where she was until Girl 6 winked at her. Girl 18 smiled as Lil yelled her name. Girl 18 followed her new boss.

Girl 6 stood. 'I got it.' She went over to the refrigerator to get Girl 18's corsage. Girl 6 felt her gloom lifting a bit. Girl 39 hadn't really understood Girl 6's connection to Angela. Like everyone else, Girl 39 had sympathized on a basic level. How could she not be moved by the kid's sad story? What Girl 39 didn't perceive was Girl 6's empathy for Angela. Girl 39 didn't know about Girl 6's dreams of falling into the lightless abyss. Girl 6 had fallen just as surely as Angela – and like Angela was critically injured – traumatized, left lifeless. But now Angela was out of the hospital. She had survived the fall. It was just a glimmer of a thought in Girl 6's head, but she started to think that maybe she too might have a chance. Maybe she too could walk away from the fall. Then Girl 6 remembered Girl 18 waiting for her 'first come' corsage, and the suggestion of hope and her good wishes for Angela slipped from her mind.

Girl 6 opened the refrigerator and looked inside. It was cluttered with white paper boxes of half-eaten Chinese food, soft drinks and a few abandoned slices of pizza. Girl 6 pushed the cartons aside and found a tall stack of corsages sitting in their plastic boxes. She looked at the flowers as the cold air of the refrigerator blew over her. Girl 6 took out a boxed corsage and closed the door.

# CHAPTER TWENTY-NINE

It was the dead of night and Girl 6 was sweating. An August heat wave was smothering the city. Girl 6 sat in front of her fan and had the windows wide open, but there were no breezes. There was no relief for her. The heat, the humidity, and the grit from the city streets stained her skin. Her breath was sludgy and thick, her body had to work hard to sustain itself. There didn't seem to be enough air, and Girl 6 felt like she was suffocating.

Girl 6 had hit bottom. Sitting in an armchair, Girl 6's dress was unzipped at the top and pulled down to her waist. The bottom of her dress was hiked up similarly to her navel. She should have just taken it off. She wanted to take it off, but didn't have the energy left to do much of anything. Earlier in the night, Girl 6 had put on the black bobbed wig of Mistress April. The hours had dislodged it, however, and it hung skewed over her head like a deluded man's hairpiece.

Outside in the hallway the pay phone rang endlessly, unanswered.

Inside, Girl 6 was about to sex the nightmarish Caller 30. He introduced himself with his usual venom.

'Hello there, it's Mr Snuff.'

'I know.' Girl 6's voice was absent of affect. It was toneless, neither happy nor sad, sexy or funny, living or dead.

Caller 30 didn't waste time with small talk. 'Are you ugly?'

Girl 6 wasn't going to agree with him. 'No, Mr Snuff, I'm beautiful.'

Caller 30 had a story to tell. 'The other day I was watching Oprah and she had a show on phone sex, and all of the girls were ugly. Are you ugly?'

Girl 6 wasn't sure if she were standing up for herself or just giving him what he wanted to hear. She didn't really know the difference anymore. 'No, I'm not ugly. I'm beautiful.'

Caller 30 played with her some more. 'You wouldn't lie to me would you? Do you miss me?'

She didn't know why, but Girl 6 chose to be honest. 'Kind of.' Girl 6 hated Caller 30 but wanted to hear more of what he had to say. Except that wasn't the entire truth. It wasn't a matter of wanting or choice anymore; she needed to hear him.

Like many sociopaths, Caller 30 had his own perverse form of brilliance. He knew precisely how to manipulate people. Caller 30 knew what they wanted to hear and knew what they needed to hear. Caller 30 led Girl 6 along – swerving back and forth between dependence and savagery. 'I've really opened up to you. I trust you.'

Girl 6 was stuck. She knew she shouldn't believe him. Yet she had to say she did. And in some way that fictional part of her had taken over – the character who was an amorphous cross between Girl 6, Lovely, Mistress April and all the others. She was no longer them. They were her.

Caller 30 stood under the decaying structure of the West Side Highway. Water from an earlier storm cascaded down the steel pillars. A car driving several stories above tossed out large plastic bags of garbage as it passed. Waste and refuse rained down, framing Caller 30 at his payphone. Down here, even the rats were nervous and they scurried frantically to their destinations. Caller 30 changed directions on Girl 6.

'I trust you – yes, I do. And now it's time for the good part.'

'I'm scared.' Girl 6's voice could barely be heard above the dull roar of traffic.

Caller 30 liked it when she was scared. He was going to reward her. 'I'll be quick and you'll be happier when it's over.'

'Okay.'

Caller 30 knew what Girl 6 was feeling. 'You're not happy now, are you?'

'No.'

Girl 6 cringed as she waited to hear more. Her face showed her anguish as she tried to balance an impossible contradiction in her head. Caller 30 knew she was weakening.

'Ya not happy because you're a fuck slut. Go on. Say it.'

'I'm a fuck slut.' Girl 6 was crying and sinking out of her chair and towards the floor.

Caller 30 was relentless – he could smell blood. 'You'll be happier once I've done this for you. We'll put yer head in a bag and tie it up good and then give you the fuck of your life – and then – lights out. Lights completely out.'

Girl 6 was screaming inside but was too spent to do anything but talk in a staggeringly flat tone. 'Why are you doing this?'

Girl 6 was falling down the empty elevator shaft. Her hands went out desperately trying to find something to hold on to, something to save her.

Caller 30 hadn't liked being asked why he did the things he did. 'That's none of your fucking business.'

'Okay.' Girl 6 was pushed back into her place by his fury.

Caller 30 wanted to ascend to the next level of his fantasy. 'Ready?'

'Yes.' She had agreed to her own murder. She had agreed to complete self-negation. Girl 6 had agreed to become nothing.

Girl 6 hit the bottom of the elevator shaft but she wasn't dead. She looked around to see what the end of the line looked like and saw a man approaching her with his hand covering his face. Girl 6 couldn't move, couldn't escape; the fall had left her paralyzed. She was trapped. The man began to slowly, ritualistically, uncover his face and reveal himself. Girl 6 waited, anxious to see who was threatening her, but, just as his face began to emerge, Girl 6's vision was cut off as he covered her face and began to smother her.

Caller 30's voice brought Girl 6 back to the moment. 'Let's spice this up some. I'm gonna come over to your house and we'll do this for real. How's that sound?'

Girl 6 was instantly alert. She sat up in her chair, her limbs weak with fear. She wanted to talk him away from this line of thought. 'It's more fun like this, baby.'

Caller 30 heard the fear in her voice. 'Bullshit. I live nearby so I'll see ya in the flesh in a sec, okay?'

Girl 6 pulled her dress down and buttoned the top. She shut off the lights in the apartment, staggered over to the window, and shut the blinds. She separated two slats and looked fearfully outside as though she could see him approaching.

Caller 30 savored her terror. 'I'll put the bag around yer head good and tight. And I'll watch you struggle.'

Girl 6 looked for safety in her anonymity. 'You don't know where I live.'

She was wrong. He did know. 'Twelve nineteen on the Avenue. See ya, bitch.'

Girl 6 ripped of her headset and let it fall to the floor as she dialed the service's switchboard. Girl 6 needed someone to change her mood. 'It's Lovely. Just got another wild card. Send someone – sweet.'

The operator knew without being told what Girl 6 had dealt with. Wild cards were always assholes. Anybody who'd bother to track a girl down had to be fucked up.

'Sit tight. I'll call ya right back.'

Girl 6 hung up. The new caller would calm her down – return her to the normal routine.

The phone started to ring and Girl 6 picked it up before it finished its first announcement. Caller 30 was on the phone. 'I'm on the corner, do you want anything?'

Girl 6 didn't know if he was for real or not. Either way it scared her. Caller 30 was someone she never wanted to meet. Girl 6 slammed the phone down, ran to the windows and locked them. As she bolted the apartment doors she knew that Caller 30 was now a part of her reality. How had she ever come to this? This wasn't her life – this wasn't anyone's fantasy, only a nightmare. Girl 6 lowered the mirror on the vanity table and dragged the whole piece of furniture until it sat protectively in front of the front door. She was safe. He couldn't get inside.

The phone rang. Girl 6 didn't touch it. After a moment she thought maybe it'd be best to try and talk him down and answered. Caller 30 had been shopping. 'I just picked up some of those blue baggies – you know, the see-through kind.'

'Leave me alone.'

Caller 30 tried another approach. 'Don't be shy. I just wanna say hey.'

Girl 6 had to frighten him off. 'My guy's gonna be home any second.'

Caller 30 could hear in her voice that she wasn't telling the truth. 'Don't lie. No one wants you but me. I'll get it around your head good and you'll be begging me for it.'

Girl 6 wasn't sure what to say any more. She went back to being compliant. 'Oh yeah, baby. That's really hot.'

Caller 30 wasn't distracted. 'Then I'll ram my thing in and have a real wild time.'

Girl 6 thought for a moment that she had brought Caller 30 back to some level of normalcy. She hadn't. Caller 30 was looking for more than a quick fuck. 'We'll have a real wild time, and then whoa, lights out. See ya in a sec, sexy 6.'

Girl 6 was terrified and furious. 'You're a sick motherfucker! You need some serious fucking help cuz you got some problems.' Girl 6 slammed the phone down.

The phone rang.

Girl 6 picked it up and slammed it back on to its cradle.

The phone rang.

Girl 6 picked it up and slammed it back on to its cradle.

The phone rang.

Girl 6 began to cry and brushed the tears away from her eyes in a panic. She lifted the phone and crushed it back on to its cradle.

The phone rang.

Girl 6 screamed quietly, a sound of despair and fear. Her

hands shook wildly as she lifted the phone and dropped the receiver. She could hear Caller 30 starting to speak. Girl 6 fell to the floor and tried to put the receiver back on to its cradle but missed her target and it fell again. She whimpered unintelligible things to block out the petrifying words from Caller 30. Girl 6 finally hung up the phone but almost pushed it off the table as she did. She barely managed to restore its balance and keep it from falling to the floor.

The phone rang.

Girl 6 was now hysterical and the noises coming from her were less than human. She sounded like a panicked animal caught in some gruesome and deadly trap. Girl 6 criedscreamedyelled and backed away irrationally from the telephone but couldn't escape from the relentless, shattering attention of Caller 30.

Jimmy was awakened by the sound of someone pounding on his door and cryingscreamingshouting his name frantically. Still wearing his pajamas, Jimmy opened the door and found Girl 6 desperate to come inside – looking like a deranged street person, looking like he had never seen her before.

'Let me in!'

Before Jimmy could reply, Girl 6 pushed her way into the apartment. Jimmy closed the door behind her. Somehow he wasn't all that surprised.

'I need to sleep with you. No, I mean I need to spend the night here. I don't feel safe in my apartment.'

Jimmy didn't have to be begged. He had strong feelings for Girl 6, but this wasn't Girl 6 – not even close. He knew the Girl 6 he wanted existed underneath all this shit though. Maybe he could bring her back to what she was. While Jimmy'd been angry with her and still was, he couldn't help but feel bad for her. He tried to make her laugh by asking the obvious in his ironic deadpan.

'This have something to do with your phone job?'

'Whatdoyouthink? Are you gonna help me out or not? Yes or no?'

Jimmy looked at her like she was an idiot. What did she think he was going to do? She might not know who the hell she was but how could she not know who he was?

Hours later Girl 6 hadn't slept. She lay next to Jimmy and thought about how fucked-up her life had become. Girl 6 knew she had reached the bottom rung on the ladder and the next step down would be into oblivion. She thought about her dreams of falling down the elevator shaft like little Angela King. And then she remembered what she had heard on her last visit to Lil's office. Angela King had been released from the hospital. She had gotten out. Girl 6 spent a long time thinking about what getting out would mean for her. What did she need to do to get out?

Jimmy lay next to her, equally sleepless. He had known Girl 6 for some time now and had thought about her constantly. Jimmy thought about doing everyday things with her and he had thought about sleeping with her. He had imagined a complete re-lationship and history with her. The games they went to, the movies they saw, the bars they drank at, the clubs they danced in, the trips they went on, the house they bought, the kids they had – all when Girl 6 made it as a star and he sold his terrifically valu-able collection of memorabilia. Now he was lying in bed next to Girl 6 and nothing had happened and nothing was going to happen. The more Jimmy had tried to predict things in his life, the more he realized that nothing really could be fixed. Things happened as they did and there wasn't much point in trying to rearrange them.

Girl 6 rolled over and looked at him. 'Jimmy? Jimmy?'

'What?' Jimmy was tired and pissed off. He didn't feel like talking.

'You asleep?'

Jimmy sighed, 'Yes.'

Girl 6 sat up in bed. She had reached a decision. 'I'm going to LA.'

Jimmy was surprised – another thing he wouldn't have been able to predict. 'I thought it was falling into the Pacific Ocean.'

Girl 6 had decided to follow Angela King's path out of the elevator shaft. She was going to walk out as best she could, on her own. 'Gonna start all over, seriously pursue my acting.'

In a way Jimmy didn't want her to go. He knew, though, that those feelings were a selfish and unrealistic take on things. He and Girl 6 would never be together. Her decision was a good one and Jimmy knew that she was doing the right thing. 'I'm happy for you.' Jimmy had reached an equally tough conclusion. They were both going to face reality straight on. 'You know I finally broke down and sold a lot of my collection, couldn't wait twenty years anymore. Gotta eat today, pay the rent.'

Jimmy got out of bed and walked to his desk. He picked up a card and sat down next to Girl 6. He handed it to her. 'I want you to have this. It's a TOPPS 1964 baseball card, mint condition. TOPPS in the National League, Willie Mays and Hank Aaron, signed by both. Be safe. Remember me.'

Girl 6 understood the gift he was giving her. Girl 6 kissed Jimmy and promised she would remember him. 'I will.'

# CHAPTER THIRTY

Girl 6 walked across the lobby of the New Amsterdam Royal and out the door. It was seven in the morning and while the sun was already high in the sky the streets were empty. Girl 6 wore high heels and carried two heavy suitcases, a cosmetics bag and a hatbox. As she struggled not to drop anything she noticed the shoplifter sitting on the stairs leading down to the street. He looked like hell, as though he had spent the entire night waiting for her on the street. The shoplifter's suit and tie looked like he had taken a shower in them. Lying next to him was a faded bouquet of wilted flowers that had been meant for Girl 6. He looked up when he saw her and smiled. Girl 6 didn't return the greeting and walked past him and down the street. The look on her face was determined – almost grim. Her bags were heavy and the heels unsteady but Girl 6 was managing.

The shoplifter called out after her. 'Ya girl Angie got out. Thought we could celebrate.'

Girl 6 didn't respond. She kept on walking. The shoplifter was part of her history – a part she was leaving behind.

The shoplifter sat on the steps and wondered if he was going to let her walk out of his life. Maybe it was best for both of them. Time to move on. The shoplifter didn't buy it. Even if she was heading somewhere with all her bags, he had to at least say goodbye. The shoplifter jumped to his feet and jogged behind her until he caught up.

Girl 6 wanted to keep right on walking. She wanted to ignore the shoplifter and get on with her life. He was persistent, however, and Girl 6 found that moving through the increasingly busy sidewalks was difficult with all of her baggage. The shoplifter kept asking to carry her bags and Girl 6 didn't even bother to acknowledge him. It wasn't until he promised not to steal her stuff that she laughed a little. She looked at him to see if he was kidding – he didn't really think that she thought he'd take her things? She had known the shoplifter a long time but even so, she couldn't tell if he was serious or fooling around. Before Girl 6 had walked five blocks downtown, the shoplifter was happily hauling her heaviest bags. Girl 6 didn't slow down her pace and the shoplifter had to work to keep up with her.

Girl 6 had some questions about the last few months. 'You ever call me?'

The shoplifter explained the problem. 'I would, but you're unlisted.'

Girl 6 looked at him and really tried to see who he was and where he was at. She hadn't bothered to do so in a long, long time.

The shoplifter knew what the look meant and tried to explain why he would have called if he could have called. 'I just wanted a regular friend-to-friend conversation. How you doing, normal stuff like that.'

Girl 6 believed the shoplifter was telling the truth – even if she also knew he would have been incapable of being just a normal everyday 'friend.' She knew that he would have tried but wouldn't have been able to keep things simple. Still, she appreciated the sincerity of his intention.

Girl 6 felt she owed the shoplifter some explanation of where she was going. 'I'm going to LA Where it's safe.'

The shoplifter was taken by surprise. He didn't understand her way of thinking. 'How in hell is LA safe? Earthquakes, floods, fires, riots and shit.'

Those seemed like easily conquered challenges to Girl 6. She had seen worse. She had seen more intimate catastrophes. 'It's safer than here. Plus I want to get my acting thing happening again.'

The shoplifter still didn't get it. Why would she go to LA where she didn't know anybody? Why would she want to start all over again? Here in New York she knew how things worked.

People – at least some people – knew who she was and knew she was a good actress. Why give that up? Why take the steps backward? The shoplifter didn't understand.

'You can't act in New York?'

'No. Not now. Too much history.' Girl 6 knew that she could never have her old life back.

The shoplifter stopped and put the bags down on the sidewalk. Girl 6 continued on for a few steps and turned around. She didn't know what the shoplifter was up to and wasn't looking forward to finding out. All she wanted to do was get out of this city. All she wanted to do was leave everyone she knew behind. The shoplifter had no scams in mind, however. He looked at Girl 6 without pretense and spoke honestly from his heart.

'Judy, I'm going to miss you Judy.'

Judy felt a bittersweet feeling overwhelm her. She tried to figure out why she felt the way she did. Judy thought carefully and tried to stay removed from her surging emotion. After a while she realized that it had been far too long since she had thought of herself as Judy. If the shoplifter had stolen things from her in the past – her heart, her dignity, her money, her peace of mind – he had just given her back, made her a gift of, the most valuable thing she had ever possessed. The shoplifter gave Judy back her identity – her self. She thanked the shoplifter. 'Judy. I always liked how you said my name.'

Judy and the shoplifter embraced deeply and kissed. It wasn't a reunion and it wasn't a farewell. It was an acknowledgement of mutual affection. It was an admission that each of them mattered – to each other and to the world. It was an acceptance of who the other one was, faults and qualities intertwined in an indecipherably complex mess of personality. In Judy's mind it was raining telephones.

She broke away from the shoplifter. 'Sam. I gotta catch a plane.' With Judy gone, maybe now Sam would break away from her label of being the shoplifter and find something new to do with his life. Judy hailed a cab and Sam put her bags in the trunk. She got into the backseat and he gently closed the door for her. The cab pulled out into the avenue and Judy sighed with relief.

# CHAPTER THIRTY-ONE

*Miss Judy Brown had been driven through the Paramount gates by her personal driver. The guards had smiled deferentially and waved her through. They knew how to behave in front of a superstar when they saw one. A receptionist met Miss Brown at the director's lavish bungalow and led her to a comfortable chair in the perfectly designed waiting area. She offered Miss Brown imported water and even a glass of wine. Miss Judy Brown wanted nothing. She took in the extravagant arrangements of freshly cut flowers, oversized paintings of exceedingly abstract human representations, and an enormous aquarium with a fish that looked like a piranha. Her working conditions had certainly improved.*

*After a few minutes a too-well-dressed male assistant scurried out of an interior office begging her to accept the director's apologies.*

*'He's so sorry to keep you waiting. He and your agents had to work out a few minor details.'*

*The assistant offered his hand and helped Miss Brown to her feet. They walked together down a stunning hallway with Mexican tiles and elaborate plantings. The assistant was trying hard to reassure Miss Brown. 'This is of course not a reading. He just wants to have a little meeting. He wants to catch up, go over the specifics.'*

*Miss Judy Brown was graciously accommodating. 'Of course.' Miss Judy Brown had learned that there was no power like not having to prove that you were powerful.*

*They were met at the office door by one of Hollywood's all-time box office champions. The director didn't have to suck up to anyone, but he felt a natural awe while in Miss Brown's presence. Miss Judy Brown basked in his sycophantic admiration. He stroked her with his voice, 'Lovely, baby, darling. Howyabeen? Let's have a look atcha. Mmmm-mmmm-mmmmm – I could eat you up. Mmmm-mmmm-mmmm.'*

'Mmmm-mmm. Now Rob, yer gonna shoot her the line . . .' Miss Judy Brown, movie star, dissolved back to reality and returned to her natural identity as Judy an unknown actress at an audition. Judy wore a plain white blouse and little makeup. She sat in a workman-like production studio a few miles north of Paramount. It wasn't the big time, it wasn't fabulous and glitzy, but it was something. The director continued with his instructions as he watched her through the video monitor. 'Rob, shoot her the line and when you answer him, honey, turn yer head real slow. Kiss. And let yer top open up and drop down like we talked about. All right? Rob – shoot. Action.'

A man in his early thirties who had a bland male-ingénue look read his line.

'Delivery.'

Judy thought she recognized the voice but couldn't place it. Judy read her line.

'Come on in.'

The director was on top of the action. 'And kiss.' Judy and Rob kissed deeply. The director was pleased. It was hot, it was gonna catch the film on fire.

'Good. Now let ya top open up. Let's see ya tits, honey. Come on. Keep the kiss going. Rob. Help her. We ain't got all year, sweetheart.'

Judy was still trying to figure out where she had heard Rob's voice before. She wasn't sure but it seemed to Judy that Rob was the voice of Caller 1 – the loser who had stood her up at Coney Island. Whether or not Rob was Caller 1 didn't matter to Judy. The director was practically drooling in anticipation of her dropping her shirt. Judy had made this mistake before. She wasn't going to do it again. Fuck the director. Fuck Rob. Fuck all these assholes who wanted her to give them something that wasn't what she was there for. She was an actress and a human being, not a piece of meat for them to jerk off to. Judy had gone too far down that road in New York. She had made a change in her life and wasn't going to accept this sort of shit anymore.

Judy looked into the confused director's camera with a newly found and hard-earned sense of determination. Judy wasn't going to lose ever again. Judy was going to be an actress and she was going to do it on her own terms. She began to perform her audition piece.

'I want you to know the only reason I'm consenting to this is because I wish to clear my name, not that I care what people think but enough is enough.'

The director hoped that she'd take off her shirt as she paused. He was disappointed. Judy became her character but didn't lose herself entirely in the role. She was still grounded in the fact that she was playing a role.

'And if in the end it helps some other people that's fine too. I consider myself normal, whatever that means. Some people call me a freak. I hate that word, I don't believe in labels. But what are you gonna do? This was the deal.'

The director waited another moment thinking that maybe now this high-brow bimbo was gonna show her tits.

Judy gathered her things together. She had auditioned. That's all they were going to get.

The director shrugged. 'No offense. We're trying to be free, no restrictions. That's what's required of the role.'

Judy didn't want to hear it and walked out of the studio without regret. As she walked through the double glass doors, Judy found herself on Hollywood Boulevard standing on the star of Marilyn Monroe. She looked around and saw the grimy cheap stores of the area and shook her head. Judy hadn't thought Hollywood would be this shabby, but then nothing really surprised her anymore. She looked west and saw the long line of Walk-of-Fame stars fading into the smoggy distance. Tourists from all over the world looked tired and bewildered. A Japanese tour group looked around in dismay – this wasn't the glory of Hollywood that they had expected. A young wandering German couple checked their map, certain they had arrived in the wrong place. They had only to look at each other to find something more appealing than the surrounding squalor and human wreckages tottering around – eaten alive by their unnurturing dreams. A tremendously fat couple from Miami posed proudly in front of the Chinese Theater as a hustler took their picture.

Judy knew better. She knew better than to have expected more. Judy was ready to begin a difficult process. She had no illusions. She knew what she wouldn't do. She knew what she had to do. Judy stepped out from the shadow of the building and made her way down Hollywood Boulevard. The harsh southern California light protected nothing and showed things for what they were. Judy didn't want it any other way. She was ready for Hollywood. She wasn't suckered by its soiled promise and she didn't flinch in front of its weary despair. Judy was stronger and tougher than she had been a year ago. Judy was ready for the role of her lifetime and called 'Action' in her head.

She walked forward down the street, joining the crowded humanity – but being only herself.

# SIGNET

*Published or forthcoming*

# IT TAKES TWO

**Maeve Haran**

Hotshot lawyer Tess Brien and her ad-man husband Stephen know that a good marriage is hard to keep. They should. Enough of their friends' relationships are crumbling around them. But theirs is a happy home, a secure base for their two lively teenagers.

But when Stephen suddenly gives up his job, leaving a stressed and angry Tess to pick up the bills, and another woman seems determined to have Stephen at any cost, distrust and disruption threaten to destroy their idyllic home ...

'Maeve Haran has a feel for the substantial concerns of her readers ... which is why she has become required reading for modern romantics' – *The Times*

*Published or forthcoming*

**SIGNET**

# BORN IN FIRE

**Sarah Hardesty**

A child of the wild, unspoilt Clare country-
side, Margaret Mary Concannon is as tough,
beautiful – and vulnerable – as the exquisite
glass sculptures she creates from sand and
flame.

Rogan Sweeney, a wealthy and sophisticated
Dubliner, is the owner of the Worldwide top
international art gallery, who can bring fame
and fortune to Maggie: if she will submit to his
terms.

But Maggie is not given to submission. Wilful,
solitary and determined to be beholden to no
one, she is drawn into a tempestuous battle with
Rogan over which of them has control of her
work, her money, her life – and her heart.

**SIGNET**

*Published or forthcoming*

# LOOSE AMONG THE LAMBS

**Jay Brandon**

In the endless heat of a San Antonio summer, three children are abducted and abused. As the city howls for justice, a man steps forward to offer his confession. An innocent man ...

District Attorney Mark Blackwell and Prosecutor Becky Schirhart get on the case and begin to peel back the complex web of lies and deceit protecting those who think they are beyond the law. Starting with their own department ...

'The pace is effortlessly sustained to produce a gripping story whose outcome is uncertain till the final pages' – *Sunday Telegraph*

*Published or forthcoming*

SIGNET

# ANGELFACE

**Lilie Ferrari**

London in the 1950s. The streets of Soho are bustling, cosmopolitan and lively. But inside the Imperial Café the Peretti family is face to face with its Sicilian enemies, who have come to call in a debt of honour incurred back in the old country.

Marionetta Peretti, although bound by the duties of an Italian daughter, despises the cowardice and caution of her family. But it is Marionetta herself who is forced to make the harshest payments: the sacrifice of her love, her freedom, and finally, herself ...

**SIGNET**

*Published or forthcoming*

# CLAWHAMMER

**Sam Llewellyn**

When George Devis's sister and her husband are shot dead before his eyes in Ethiopia, leaving Devis with two orphaned nephews and an unassuageable guilt, he can't do less than agree to a US fund-raising tour on their behalf. But when he is almost killed too, it's clear that funds aren't all he's raising.

And Devis only has one choice: sink, or swim.

'A lethal mix of adventure and suspense' – Bernard Cornwell

SIGNET

*Published or forthcoming*

# ROSEMARY'S BABY

**Ira Levin**

## When the truth is more sinister than imagination ...

Rosemary and Guy Woodhouse's new apartment in the Bramford was everything the young couple wanted. Yet as soon as they'd signed the lease Rosemary began to have doubts.

The neighbours were quaint but friendly. Too friendly. Especially after Mr and Mrs Castavet learned that Rosemary was planning to have a baby.

'A darkly brilliant tale of modern devilry that induces the reader to believe the unbelievable. I believed it and was altogether enthralled' – Truman Capote

'This horror story will grip you and chill you' – *Daily Express*

'Diabolically good ... the pay-off is so fiendish it made me sweat' – *Sun*

'A terrifying book ... I can think of no other in which fear of an unknown evil strikes with greater chill' – *Daily Telegraph*

*Published or forthcoming*

**SIGNET**

# Hidden Riches

**Nora Roberts**

**An actress turned antique dealer, Dora Conway believes in living life to the full.**

When Dora rents out the empty apartment above her thriving antiques shop to Jed Skimmerhorn, she gets more than she bargained for. An ex-cop with an aching secret buried in his past, Jed will push the world away rather than risk more pain.

Her curiosity aroused by Jed, Dora suddenly finds herself swept into another dangerous mystery – and one that has at its heart the powerful forces of money and obsession. But when she realizes that she has become someone's prey, the danger has already come too close to home ...

*Published or forthcoming*

**SIGNET**

# BLESSING IN DISGUISE

**Eileen Goudge**

**Each family is different in its unhappiness ... and its secrets.**

No one knew that better than Grace Truscott who, as a ten-year-old girl, had been a witness to an act of shocking violence that blew her family apart ... and forced her to keep a terrible secret.

From fast-paced New York to the magnolia-scented gardens of Georgia, *Blessing in Disguise* is the powerful, passionate story of a woman crossed in love and a family in search of reconciliation and forgiveness.